'*Our* son. I intend taking him to Sicily, E⸺ —and trying to stop me will seriously b⸺ e against you in the long run.'

H⸺ o his feet, moving as silently as a jungle cat to st⸺ d ⸺ ctly in front of her before continuing. 'I already ⸺ a team of lawyers working on the case, and let me ⸺ you that they ⸺ ere singularly unimpressed by your eff⸺ s to conceal ⸺ y son from me.'

Emma s⸺ llowed. 'You're threatening me— I—'

But her ⸺ s were halted by the soft dig of Vincenzo's fingers ⸺ her arms as he hauled her to her feet. 'I am taking ⸺ ⸺ with me, and if you intend to accompany us then yo⸺ ⸺ play the part of my wife.'

She ⸺ p at him. It was as if she had slipped and was fa⸺ g d⸺ er and deeper into a dark hole of Vincenzo's ⸺ g. '⸺ ur *wife*?'

⸺ eyes burned into her. 'Why not? It makes perfect s⸺ .' He saw the look of confusion darkening her blue e⸺ 'We might as well enjoy what pleasures we can w⸺ we have the opportunity to do so.'

E⸺ a felt weak. He sounded so cold-blooded—as if p⸺ re were nothing more than the by-product of a ⸺ function. 'You can't mean that.'

⸺ ⸺ t I can,' he promised, with grim satisfaction. ⸺ think you could usefully lose the outraged attitude, don't you? In view of your response to me, you're in danger of looking a little like a ~~hypocrite.~~

'⸺ ⸺

'⸺ ⸺ played a⸺ ⸺ a, and n⸺

Sharon Kendrick started story-telling at the age of eleven and has never really stopped. She likes to write fast-paced, feel-good romances, with heroes who are so sexy they'll make your toes curl! Born in west London, she now lives in the beautiful city of Winchester—where she can see the cathedral from her window (but only if she stands on tiptoe). She has two children, Celia and Patrick, and her passions include music, books, cooking and eating—and drifting off into wonderful daydreams while she works out new plots!

SICILIAN HUSBAND, UNEXPECTED BABY

BY

SHARON KENDRICK

First published in Great Britain 2008
Harlequin Mills & Boon Limited,
Eton House, 18-24 Paradise Road, Richmond, Surrey TW9 1SR

© Sharon Kendrick 2008

ISBN: 978 0 263 86476 2

Set in Times Roman 10½ on 12¾ pt
01-1108-43691

Printed and bound in Spain
by Litografia Rosés, S.A., Barcelona

SICILIAN HUSBAND, UNEXPECTED BABY

To Janet, Barbara and Allen, with love.

CHAPTER ONE

EMMA felt the frisson of very real fear sliding over her skin. She looked at the lanky blond man standing in front of her and composed her face carefully—because the last thing she could afford to do was panic.

'But I can't afford any more rent, Andrew,' she said quietly. 'You know that.'

The man shrugged apologetically but his expression didn't change. 'And I'm not running a charity. I'm sorry, Emma—but I could get four times the amount I'm charging you if I put it back on the market.'

Like a robot, Emma nodded. Of course he could. Pretty little cottages in pretty little English towns were snapped up like hot cakes. Everyone, it seemed, was into rural living these days.

The man hesitated. 'Isn't there anyone you could ask? Anyone who could help? What about your husband?'

Quickly, Emma stood up, fixing a crumpled attempt at a smile to her lips and wondering if it fooled anyone. Just the very mention of the man she had married had the power to make her feel weak, but weakness had no place in her life, not any more. She simply couldn't afford to let it. 'It's very kind of you to be concerned, but it's my problem,' she said.

'Emma—'

'Please, Andrew,' she said, trying to keep her voice calm—because she never spoke of Vincenzo, not to anyone. 'Either I come up with the increased rent or I move somewhere cheaper—those are the only two solutions open to me.'

She knew there was also an unacknowledged third— Andrew had made that very clear in that sweet and polite English way of his. But she wasn't going to start dating him just to keep her rent at a below-market-rate level, and, anyway, she didn't want a boyfriend. She didn't want anyone in her life—she had no room, no time or inclination for a man. And desire had died in her the day she had left Vincenzo.

Andrew said goodbye, disappearing into the dank November air just as a whimper came from the small bedroom and Emma crept in to stare at her sleeping son.

Already ten months old—how was that possible? He was growing in leaps and bounds with every day that passed—developing his own sturdy little frame to go along with his very definite personality.

He had kicked his duvet away and was clutching his little woollen rabbit as if his life depended on it and Emma's heart turned over with love and worry. If there had been just her to think about, then there wouldn't have been a problem. There were plenty of jobs available which came with a room and she would gladly have taken any one of them.

But it wasn't just her. There was her son to think about—and she owed him the very best that the world could provide. It wasn't his fault that his birth had placed her in an impossible situation.

Emma bit her lip. She knew what Andrew had suggested made sense, but it wasn't as easy as that—and Andrew didn't know the details. Nobody did. Could she really swallow her pride and her beliefs and go to her cstranged husband, asking him for financial assistance?

Was she perhaps due some, by law? Vincenzo was a fabulously wealthy man and—even though he now despised her and had told her he never wanted to see her again—wouldn't he play fair by providing her with some kind of modest settlement if she asked him for a divorce?

Tiredly, she rubbed at her eyes. What other solution did she have? She wasn't qualified for anything high-earning and the last time she'd gone out to work had ended up paying most of her meagre wages to the child-minder. And little Gino had hated it.

So she'd taken up child-minding herself. It had seemed the perfect compromise—she loved children and it was a way of earning money to pay the bills without having to farm out her beloved son to anyone else while she did so. But lately even that avenue of employment had caved in.

Several of the mothers had complained that her cottage

was too cold for their children and demanded that she increase the temperature significantly. Two even removed their children straight away and her suspicions that there was going to be a domino effect and that the rest would follow suit were soon proved true. Now there were no more children to look after and no money coming in.

How on earth was she going to feed herself and Gino? Put a roof over their heads if Andrew increased the rent? Emma wanted to cry but she knew that she could not afford the luxury of tears—and tears would solve precisely nothing. There was nobody to dry them except for her and tears were for babies—except that she was determined her little boy was going to cry as little as possible. She had to be the grown-up now.

Opening the drawer of the small telephone table, she extracted the well-worn business card—her hand beginning to shake as she stared down at the name which leapt out at her like a dark crow from the sky.

Vincenzo Cardini.

Beneath it were the contact details of his offices in Rome, New York and Palermo—which she could never afford to ring in a month of Sundays—but also the number of his London offices, which she assumed he still operated out of regularly.

And yet it hurt to think that he might still own a luxurious tower block in the capital. To realise that he might have spent long and regular amounts of time in the same country as her and not once—*not once*—bothered to come and look her up, not even for old times' sake.

Well, of course he wouldn't, she scolded herself. *He doesn't love you any more, he doesn't even like you— he made that quite plain. Remember his last words for you—delivered in that deadly cold, Sicilian drawl of his.*

'Get out of here, Emma and do not come back—for you are no wife of mine.'

But hadn't she tried to ring him before, not once, but twice—and both times hadn't he humiliatingly refused to speak to her? What was to say that this time would be any different?

Yet she knew she owed it to her son to keep trying. She owed him the right to know something of the basic comfort which should be every child's entitlement and which his father's money could guarantee. Wasn't that more important than anything else? She needed to do this for Gino's sake.

Emma shivered, pulling her sweater closer to her slim frame. These days her clothes seemed to swallow her up. She generally wore layers and kept on the move in this chilly autumn weather to keep herself warm. But soon her son would be awake and then she would have to put the heating on and more of her precious pennies would be eaten up by the ever-hungry gas fire.

There was, she realised heavily, no choice other than to ring Vincenzo. Running her tongue around her suddenly parched lips, she lifted up the phone and punched out the number with a shaky finger, her accelerated heart rate making her feel dizzy with expectation.

'Hello?' The voice of the woman who answered

was smooth and with only a trace of an accent, probably bilingual.

But Vincenzo only employed people who could speak Italian, as well as English, Emma remembered. He even preferred it if his employees also spoke the very particular Sicilian dialect—which was a mystery to so many. Because Sicilians looked out for one another, he had once told her. They were members of a unique club of which they were fiercely proud. In fact, the more Emma thought about it, the more surprising she found it that he had ever chosen to marry her at all—she who spoke nothing more than a smattering of anything other than her native tongue.

He married you because he felt obliged to, she reminded herself. *And didn't he tell you that enough times? Just as the marriage broke down because you were unable to keep your part of the bargain.*

'Hello?' said the woman's voice again.

'Would it be…?' Emma cleared her throat. 'Er, could you tell me how I could get hold of Signor Cardini, please?'

There was a short silence—as if the telephonist was shocked that a faltering unknown should dare to ask to be put through to the great man himself.

'May I ask who is calling?'

Emma took a deep breath. *Here we go.* 'My name is…Emma Cardini.'

There was another pause. 'And your call is in connection with…?'

So there was no recognition of her name and no knowledge of her status. No respect, either—and something deep inside Emma bristled with hurt and rejection.

'I'm his wife,' she said baldly.

The woman had clearly been wrong-footed and Emma could almost hear her thinking—*What the hell do I tell her?*

'Please hold the line,' she said crisply.

Emma was forced to wait for what seemed like an eternity, while pinpricks of sweat beaded her forehead despite the chilly atmosphere in the cottage. She was just silently practising saying *Hello, Vincenzo* over and over in her head to make it sound as emotionless as possible, when the telephonist's voice broke into her thoughts.

'Signor Cardini says to tell you that he is in a meeting and cannot be disturbed.'

The humiliation hit her like a blow to the solar plexus and Emma found herself gripping on to the receiver as if she wanted to crush it in her clammy palm. She was just about to drop it back down onto the cradle when she realised the woman was still speaking to her.

'But he says if you would care to leave a number where you can be contacted, he will endeavour to ring you when he has a moment.'

Pride made Emma want to pass on the message that he could go to hell if he couldn't even be bothered to speak to the woman he had married.

But she could not afford the luxury of pride. 'Yes, here's my number,' she said quietly. 'Do you have a pen?'

'Of course,' said the woman in an amused voice.

After she had put the phone down, Emma went to make a cup of tea, cupping the steaming mug around her cold fingers as she looked out of the kitchen window at the little garden she had grown to love.

Shiny brown conkers from a large tree on Andrew's huge adjoining estate had fallen over the flint wall and all over her tiny lawn and path. She had planned to put one of those mini sandpits in an unused corner of the plot and to grow a fragrant white jasmine to scent the long summer evenings—but all those dreams seemed to be fast evaporating.

Because that was another downside she hadn't even considered until now. If she was forced to move from this rural idyll—where would her little boy play when he eventually started to toddle and then to walk? Very few cheap lets came with their own garden.

The ringing of the telephone shattered her troubled thoughts and Emma snapped it up before it could wake the baby.

'Hello?'

'*Ciao*, Emma.'

The words hit her like a bucket of ice-water. He said her name like no one else—but then, nothing that Vincenzo did or said was remotely like anyone else. He was unique—like a rare black glittering gem with dark danger at its very core.

Remember the way you've been practising saying his name in that bland and neutral way? Well, now is the time to put it into practice. 'Vincenzo.' She swallowed. 'It was good of you to call back.'

At the other end of the phone, Vincenzo's hard lips twisted into a cruel parody of a smile. She spoke as if she were about to purchase a computer from him! In that soft English voice which used to drive him crazy—both in and out of bed. And despite the still-raw hostility of his feelings for her—even now he could feel the slow coil of awareness beginning to unfurl in his groin.

'I found a brief window in my schedule,' he said carelessly, flicking his dark gaze in the direction of the crammed diary which lay open on his desk. 'What do you want?'

In spite of having told herself that she didn't care what he thought of her any more, Emma was woman enough to know a painful pang of regret. He spoke to her with less regard than he might use to someone who was removing the garbage from his house. How quickly the fires of passion could become cold grey embers which just left a dirty trace behind.

So answer him in the same matter-of-fact way—keep this brisk and formal and it might not hurt so much. 'I want a divorce.'

There was a pause. A long pause. Eyes narrowing, Vincenzo leaned back in his chair, stretching his long legs out in front of him as he considered her statement. 'Why? Have you met someone else?' he questioned coolly. 'Perhaps planning on remarrying?'

His indifference pierced her—wounded her far more

than it should have done. Could this possibly be the same Vincenzo who had once threatened to tear the limbs from a man who had asked her to dance, until she had calmed him down and told him that she had no desire to dance with any other man than him. No, of course it wasn't. That Vincenzo had loved her—or, at least, had claimed to have loved her.

'Even if I had met someone—I can assure you that I wouldn't be taking a trip down the aisle. You've put me off marriage for a lifetime, Vincenzo,' she said, wanting to try to hurt him back—but it was clearly a waste of time because his responding laugh was laced with cynicism.

'Which doesn't answer my question, Emma,' he persisted silkily.

Emma's heart missed a beat. 'And…I don't have to answer it.'

'You think not?' Vincenzo swung round in his chair and gazed out at the London skyline—at the spectacular sparkling skyscrapers which dominated it, two of which he owned. 'Well, in that case, this conversation isn't going to get very far, is it?'

'We don't need to have a *conversation*, Vincenzo, we need—'

'We need to establish facts.' His words iced into hers. 'Do you have your diary?'

'My diary?'

'Let's fix up a date to meet and talk about it.'

In the little cottage, Emma's knees sagged and she clutched onto the table for support. 'No!'

'No?' Now there was amusement in his voice as he heard the sudden panic in her voice. 'You really think that I intend to have this discussion about the end of my marriage on the *phone*?'

'There's no need for face-to-face contact—we can do it all through lawyers,' Emma ventured.

'Then go ahead and do it,' he retaliated.

Was he calling her bluff because somehow he suspected she was in a weak position? But he *couldn't* know that.

'If you want my co-operation then I suggest you meet me halfway, Emma,' Vincenzo continued softly. 'Otherwise you could have a very long and very expensive fight on your hands.'

Emma closed her eyes, willing herself not to cry—because he would seize on any outward sign of weakness like a vulture picking over a carcass. How could she have forgotten about that iron-hard resolve of his, that stubborn determination to get exactly what it was he wanted?

'Why would you fight me, Vincenzo?' she questioned wearily. 'When both of us know this marriage is dead and neither one of us wants it to continue?'

Perhaps if she had shed a tear, perhaps if her voice had wavered with just one tiny shiver of emotion—then Vincenzo might have spared her. But her cool, down-to-earth manner sparked in him a fury which had lain dormant since their marriage had broken down—and now he felt it spring into powerful and ugly life within him. At that moment, Vincenzo didn't really know or care what it was that *he* wanted—all he knew was that he wanted to thwart Emma's desires.

'Can you do Monday?' he queried, as if she hadn't spoken.

Blinking back the slight saltiness at the backs of her eyes, Emma didn't need to look in her diary—she didn't even have one. Why would she? Her social life was non-existent these days and that was the way she liked it.

'Monday seems to be…okay,' said Emma, as if she, too, had a rare *window* in her schedule. 'What time?'

'Where are you living? Can you do dinner?'

She thought about it—the last train back to Boisdale from London left just after eleven, but what if she missed it? Her friend Joanna would be happy to have Gino during the day, but taking him overnight would involve a little more juggling. Besides, she had never been apart from her baby boy for a night and she didn't intend to start now.

Ignoring the first part of his question, Emma forced herself to sound casual. 'Not dinner, no.'

'Why? Are you busy in the evening?' he mocked.

'I don't live in London. It's…easier if we do lunchtime.'

Vincenzo stretched as a glossy brunette in a close-fitting pencil skirt wiggled in to place a cup of espresso on the desk in front of him and he smiled, pausing while he watched the pert thrust of her buttocks as she sashayed out of the office. The smile left his lips. '*Sì*, then we will make it lunch,' he said softly. 'I'll have

someone fix us something here. Come to my office—
can you remember how to get here?'

But Emma baulked at the thought of going to his
London headquarters—with its gleaming magnificence
taunting her about the crazy inequality of their two life-
styles. And his office wasn't neutral territory, was it?
Vincenzo would have the upper hand—and there was
nothing he liked more.

'Wouldn't you prefer it if we went out to a…
restaurant?'

Once again Vincenzo thought he detected the waver
of hope in her voice and he was surprised at the dark
pleasure which washed over him as he swamped it. 'No,
I don't want to go to a restaurant,' he negated silkily. And
be constrained by the table between them, the hovering
of waiters and the formality of the atmosphere? No way.
'Be here at one.'

And then to Emma's disbelief he terminated the connection and she was left listening to an empty dialling
tone. Slowly, she replaced the receiver and as she
glanced up caught a glimpse of herself in the small mirror which hung over the phone. Her hair looked lank,
her face as white as chalk and there were dark circles
beneath her eyes. And Vincenzo had always been so particular how he wanted her to look—she had been his
little doll.

Although he was Sicilian, he had happily adopted the
Italian ideal of *la bella figura*—the importance of
image—of making the best of yourself. Biting her lip,

she imagined the contempt in those mocking black eyes if he could see her now. And any contempt would surely put her at even more of a disadvantage.

Between now and Monday, she was going to have to do something drastic about her appearance.

CHAPTER TWO

HEART slamming against her ribcage, Emma stared up at the Cardini building, willing herself to have the courage to walk in. It was a beautiful structure—sleek and curved and fashioned almost entirely from glass. Its design had won awards and it screamed wealth from every polished pane, throwing her reflection back at her a hundred times over and seeming to emphasise her impoverished state in this wealthy area of London.

She'd had a nightmare time trying to find something suitable to wear—all her clothes were practical, not smart—and none of them was of the delicious costly quality which had become second nature to her as Vincenzo's wife.

In the end she'd chosen a plain dress, which she had jazzed up with a bright, clumpy necklace, and had polished her boots until she could see her face in them. Only her coat was good and you could tell—soft dark cashmere lined with violet silk which felt so delicious against her spare frame. Tiny, embroidered violet flowers were scattered along the hem of the expensive material, as if someone had flung a handful of flowers there, and they had stuck. Vincenzo had bought her that coat from one of Milan's costliest shops, slipping out from their hotel one afternoon, leaving her asleep and tousled in bed, to return with a large, ribbon-wrapped box.

She hadn't wanted to wear it today—it was too full of memories, too much a slice of the past. But it was warm and, more importantly, it was smart enough to take her anywhere. And what was the alternative? To waltz into the Cardini headquarters wearing her bargain faux-fur trimmed coat—the kind of which was usually snapped up by hard-up students?

Turning dizzily in the revolving doors, Emma entered the vast, airy foyer and walked up to the reception desk—a journey which seemed to take for ever.

The Madonna behind the desk gave her a bland smile. 'May I help you?'

'I have…I have an appointment with Signor Cardini.'

The woman glanced down at a list. 'Emma Cardini?'

'That's me,' agreed Emma, thinking that the Madonna couldn't quite hide her look of surprise.

A perfectly polished pink fingernail was pointed to the far end of the foyer. 'Take the elevator to the very top of the building and someone will be waiting there to meet you.'

'Thanks.'

As the lift shot silently upwards Emma thought how long it had been since she'd visited London—and how long it had been since she'd been out without her son. And never for a whole day, like this. Would he be okay? she wondered for the hundredth time since buying her ticket at Boisdale station. Or would he kick up when he realised that his mother was gone for more than an hour or two?

Pulling the pay-as-you-go cell phone from her handbag, she stared at the blank screen. No messages. She'd told Joanna to call her if she was worried about anything—*anything*—which meant that all must be well.

So do what you have to do, she thought, drawing a deep breath as the lift pinged to a halt and the doors slid open to reveal a glamorous brunette in a close-fitting pencil skirt and a blouse which was obviously pure silk. Her hair was piled artfully on top of her head, there were two starry diamonds sparkling at her ears, and suddenly Emma felt like a poor country cousin who had come visiting. Just how many beautiful women did Vincenzo need working for him?

'Signora Cardini?' asked the woman. 'Will you please follow me? Vincenzo's expecting you.'

Well, of course he's expecting me! Emma wanted to shout as she watched the woman wiggling her way towards a set of double doors. *And who gave you the right to call my husband by his Christian name in that gurgling and rather pathetic way?*

But he's not going to be your husband for very much longer, is he? And in fact, he hasn't been your husband for a long time—so better lose the unreasonable jealousy right now, Emma.

The doors were being opened with the kind of flourish which seemed to indicate that she was being summoned into the presence of someone terribly important and Emma braced herself for the sight of Vincenzo, just as she had been doing during the journey here. But nothing could prepare her for the heart-stopping reality of seeing her husband again in the living and breathing flesh.

He was standing in front of the wall of glass which ran along one side of his arena-sized office—and so at first sight he was in silhouette. But the darkened outline only served to emphasise a physique which was utterly magnificent—all lean, honed muscle—the kind of perfection which sculptors had been using as the masculine ideal since the beginning of time.

His hands were splayed rather arrogantly over narrow hips, which tapered down to long, lean legs—but then arrogance had always been Vincenzo's middle name. He saw what he wanted and he took what he wanted—and he usually got it by a mixture of power and persuasion and sheer charisma.

Emma swallowed—the reminder pushing her into protective mode—because she had one most precious thing which Vincenzo could not be allowed to take and she needed all her wits about her.

'Hello, Vincenzo,' she said.

'Emma,' he responded, in a tone she had never heard him use before. Firing off a command in rapid Italian, which caused the brunette to quickly leave the office, closing the doors behind her, he stepped from the shad-

ow and into the light and, in spite of everything, Emma
felt her stomach turn quite weak as she looked up into
his face.

For he was even more devastatingly gorgeous than she
remembered when she had agreed to marry him. Back
then she had been carried along by the wild and dizzy
excitement of being in love—so enraptured that she had
not stopped to think that he was a truly remark-
able-looking man. And then, when the marriage had
begun to crumble, he had seemed cold, icy, uncaring—
and she had shrunk from him and he from her.

But since then Emma had been through a lot—and a
lot of it had been difficult. These days she was under no
illusion that she had briefly dallied with a dream—and
today Vincenzo looked like every woman's dream man.

He was dressed for business, in one of those amazingly
cut suits which managed to be both formal and yet not in
the least bit stuffy and could only have been made in Italy.
He'd removed his jacket, revealing a white silk shirt
which gave a tantalising hint of the rock-hard body which
lay beneath. And he'd loosened his tie, too, and undone
the top couple of buttons on his shirt, so that she could
just discern the dark whorls of hair which grew there.

But it was his face which mesmerised most, and
Emma allowed her gaze to reach it almost reluctantly—
as if dreading the impact it was going to have on her.
And it hit her with a painful shock as she realised she
was looking into a hardened and cynical version of
Gino's soft little features.

Had Vincenzo ever looked that soft and approach-able? Emma wondered as her eyes drank him in with a greed she couldn't quite suppress.

He would have been almost classically beautiful were it not for the fact that a tiny scar made a pale V-shape in the dark texture of his shadowed jaw. And his face was hard, too, with black eyes glittering like jet and a smile which was edged with a kind of cruelty. Even when he had been in hot pursuit of her, he had always had that hard edge to him. A quality which had always made her slightly wary of him.

For he had always treated her with a kind of autocratic authority. She had just been another possession to acquire along the way—the virgin bride who had never managed to follow through with what his expectations of her were.

'It has been a long time,' Vincenzo said, and his voice sounded as bitter as unripe lemons. 'Here, let me take your coat.'

She wanted to tell him that she wouldn't be staying long enough to need to take it off, but he might prove to be difficult if she did that. What was more, she had agreed to have lunch with him and the central heating in the office meant that the coat was impractical. But the last thing she wanted was Vincenzo slipping the garment from her shoulders, his hands brushing against her vulnerable skin, the very gesture reminding her of so many undressings in the past....

'I can manage,' she said, wriggling out of the coat and hanging it awkwardly over the back of a chair.

Vincenzo was studying her with an air of fascination. He had recognised the coat immediately but the dress was new—and what a horrible little dress it was. His lips curved. 'What in *Dio*'s name have you been doing to yourself?'

'What do you mean?' With an effort she kept her voice steady, trying to quell the fear that he might somehow have found out about Gino. But he couldn't have done or he wouldn't have been staring at her with that oddly distasteful look on his face. Not even he was that good an actor.

'You've been on one of those crash diets?' he demanded.

'No.'

'But you are too thin. Much too thin.'

That was what long-term breast-feeding did—she'd only stopped a couple of months ago—and if you threw in child-minding, gardening, cleaning, cooking, shopping and generally juggling her busy life without anyone else to help her, it was no wonder she'd lost serious amounts of weight.

'All skin and bone,' he continued, still in that same critical drawl.

Maybe she should have been insulted at his bald words for this was the man who used to tell her that she was a pocket Venus, that she had the most perfect body he'd ever seen on a woman. At least this way, his undisguised censure reassured Emma that the relationship really *was* dead—that, not only did he not like her, but it seemed that he did not desire her any more, either.

And yet that hurt. More than hurt. It made her feel less than a woman in all ways. A poor, desperate woman with her cheap clothes hanging off her—who had come crawling to her overbearing husband, clutching on to her begging bowl.

Well, you're not. You're simply seeking something which is rightfully yours. So don't let him wear you down.

'How I choose to look is my business, but I see you've lost nothing of your charm and diplomacy, Vincenzo,' she said tightly.

Reluctantly, Vincenzo gave a short laugh. Had he forgotten that she could give as good as she got? Hadn't that been one of the things which had first drawn him to her? Her strange kind of shyness coupled with the occasional ability to hit the nail bang on the head. Along with her ethereal blonde looks, which had completely blown him away. Well, if he met her *now*, he certainly wouldn't be blown away.

'You just look very…different,' he observed. Her hair was longer than he remembered—she used to always keep it cut to just below her shoulders and he had approved of that because it meant that it never tumbled over her beautiful breasts when she was naked. But now it fell almost to her tiny waist and looked in good need of a trim.

And her blue eyes appeared almost hollow, the sharpness of her cheekbones shadowing her face. But it was her body which shocked him most of all. She had tiny bones, but these had always been covered with firm flesh so that she was lusciously curved, like a small, ripe peach. Yet now there was a leanness about her which might be currently fashionable, but was not attractive. Not at all.

His damning assessment made Emma desperately want to draw his attention away from her. 'Whereas you look exactly the same, Vincenzo.'

'Do I?' He watched her, as a cat might watch a tiny mouse before it struck out with its lethal claws.

She flicked her gaze to his temples. 'Well, perhaps there are a couple more grey hairs.'

'Doesn't that make me look distinguished?' he mocked. 'Tell me, exactly how long *has* it been since we last saw one another, *cara*?'

She suspected he knew exactly how long it was, but instinct and experience told her to play along with him. *Don't anger or rile him. Keep him on side. Keep bland and impartial and thin and unattractive and hopefully he'll be glad to see the back of you.* 'Eighteen months. Time…flies, doesn't it?'

'Tempus volat,' he echoed softly in Italian—and indicated one of a pair of chic, leather sofas which sat at right angles to each other at the far end of the large office. 'Indeed it does. Have a seat.'

Sitting down also implied staying longer than she might wish, but Emma's knees by now were so weak with the swirl of conflicting emotions that she felt they might buckle if she didn't. She sank into the soft comfort of the seat and watched warily as he sat down next to her.

His presence unnerved and unsettled her as it had always done—but wouldn't she look weak and pathetic if she primly asked him to sit elsewhere? As if she couldn't cope with the reality of his proximity. And wasn't that another reason for coming here today—to demonstrate to him *and to herself* that what little they'd had between them was now dead?

Is it? she asked herself. Is *it*? *Of course it is, you little fool—don't even go there*.

'I'll ring for food, shall I?' he questioned.

'I'm not hungry.'

He stared at her. Neither was he—even though he had risen at six that morning and eaten only a little bread with his coffee. He thought how pale her skin looked—so translucent that he could see the fine blue tracery of veins around her temple. She wore no jewellery, he observed. Not those little pearl studs she used to favour and not her wedding ring, either. Of course. His mouth twisted. 'So let's get down to business, Emma—and, since you instigated this meeting, you must tell me what it is you want.'

'Exactly what I told you over the phone—or tried to. I want a divorce.'

His black eyes flicked over her, noticing the way that she crossed and uncrossed her legs, as if she was nervous. What was she nervous about? Seeing him again? Still wanting him? Or something else. 'And your reasons?'

Distractedly, Emma raked her hand back through her hair—then turned to him with appeal in her eyes, steeling herself against the impact of his hard, beautiful face. 'Isn't the fact that we've been separated all this time reason enough?'

'Not really, no. There is usually,' Vincenzo observed softly, 'a reason why a woman should wish to disturb the status quo for they are notoriously sentimental about marriage—even if it was a bad marriage, as in our case.'

Emma flinched. It was one thing knowing it, but quite another hearing him saying it again so cold-bloodedly. And she had seriously underestimated what an intelligent man he was. Clever enough to realise that she wouldn't just turn up out of the blue, asking for a divorce, unless there was a reason behind it. *So give him the kind of reason* he *can believe in.* 'I should have thought that you'd be glad enough to have your freedom back?'

'Freedom for what, precisely, *cara*?' he drawled.

Say it, she told herself. *Say it even if it chokes you up inside to have to say it. Confront your demons and they will disturb you no more. You've both moved on. You've had to. And the future will obviously involve different partners—especially for Vincenzo.* 'The freedom to see other women, perhaps.'

A lazy and faintly incredulous look made his ebony eyes gleam and he gave a soft laugh. 'You think I need an official termination of our marriage to do that?' he mocked. 'You think that I have been living like a monk since you left me?'

Despite the lack of logic in her response, Emma's lips fell open in dismay as disturbing visual images lanced through her mind like a sharp knife. 'You've been sleeping with other women?' she questioned painfully.

'What do you think?' he taunted. 'Although you flatter me by presuming numbers—'

'And you flatter yourself with your false modesty, Vincenzo!' Emma said in a low voice. 'Since we both know you can get any woman to come running with a click of your fingers.'

'Like I got you, you mean?'

Emma bit her lip. *Don't destroy my memories*, she pleaded silently. 'Don't rewrite history. You came after me. You wooed me,' she protested in a low voice. 'You know you did.'

'On the contrary, you played a game,' he demurred. 'You were far cleverer than I gave you credit for, Emma. You played the innocent quite perfectly—'

'Because I *was* innocent!' she declared.

'And that, of course, was your trump card,' he murmured. Vincenzo leaned back against the sofa, arrogantly letting his gaze drift up her legs and over her thighs, which the cheap fabric of her dress was clinging to like cream. 'You played your virginity like a champion, didn't you? You saw me, you wanted me and you teased me so alluringly that I was unable to resist you. You saw me as a man who had everything—a Sicilian who would value your purity above all else and be bound by it!'

'I...*didn't*...' she breathed.

'So why didn't you tell me you were a virgin before it was too late?' he snapped. 'I would never have touched you if I'd known!'

She wanted to tell him that she had been so in awe of him and so in love with him and that was why the subject hadn't come up. That things had rocketed out of control. She had been at an utterly vulnerable time in her life and had thought him way out of her league—hadn't for a moment thought that the affair would progress through to marriage. Hadn't he told her—fiercely and ardently—that he would one day marry a woman from his homeland, who would inculcate their children with the same values they had grown up with?

And yet on some far deeper level she *had* known that he would have run a mile if he'd been aware that she was a virgin—but, of course, by then she had been in too deep to be able to withstand the hungry demands of her body and her heart to risk telling him.

'I wanted you to be my first lover,' she told him truthfully. Because she had suspected that no other man who came into her life would ever come close to Vincenzo.

Vincenzo's lips curled in derision. 'You wanted a rich husband!' he stated disparagingly. 'You were all alone in the world with no qualifications, no money and no property—and you saw your wealthy Sicilian as a ticket to ride your sweet little body out of poverty.'

'That's not true!' said Emma, stung.

'Isn't it?' he challenged.

Colour flared into her cheeks. 'I'd have married you if you'd had nothing.'

'But fortunately for you it never came to that, did it, *cara*?' he retorted sarcastically. 'Since you already knew what I was worth.'

Emma flinched as if he had hit her—but in a way his words were more wounding than physical blows could ever be. *At least you know now what he thinks of you*, she thought to herself. But she was damned if he would see her break down in front of him. She would get what she came for and she would walk out of here with her head held high.

'Well, in view of what you've just said—at least neither of us can be in any doubt that seeking a divorce is the only sensible solution,' she said calmly.

Vincenzo stilled and something inside him rankled. He didn't like it when she used logic—it made her seem untouchable again and he was used to women always being passionate around him. So was Emma really immune to him—as unbothered by the idea of legally ending their marriage as she seemed—or was it all an act? Would she still turn on for him? he wondered idly.

Completely without warning, he leaned over her, almost negligently brushing his lips over hers, and smiled with triumph as he felt their automatic tremble at that briefest of touches.

Emma froze, even as she felt the blood beginning to

heat her skin and the sudden mad thunder of her heart. 'Vincenzo,' she whispered. 'What the hell do you think you're doing?'

CHAPTER THREE

'JUST testing,' Vincenzo murmured, and returned his mouth to Emma's, feeling her rapid breath warming his lips, and he found he wanted to lick his way into her—every part of her—as he had done so many times before.

'Don't—'

But she wasn't pushing him away, was she? He could sense, almost smell Emma's desire for him—but then he had always been able to read her like some long and erotic book. At least until the relationship had withered away to such an extent that they could hardly bear to look one another in the eye, let alone touch one another....

Until that very last time. Just before she had walked out of the door into the blazing Roman heat—he had caught her to him and had begun to kiss her and she had kissed him back, angrily and with more passion than she'd shown for months.

He remembered rucking up her little skirt and pushing aside her panties and pushing into her: doing it to her upright against the wall, where she stood. Remembered her gasping her orgasm in his ear. And then, ignoring her protests that she would miss her flight, he had carried her up to their bedroom. To the bed they had not shared for weeks—and had spent that one long, last sleepless night imprinting himself on her body and her mind. Pulling out every sensual skill he had ever learnt and using them on her almost ruthlessly as she had moaned with pleasure and regret.

Dio, he was getting hard now just thinking about it. Too hard.

'Emma,' he ground out, and this time his lips didn't brush hers. They crushed them beneath his as ruthlessly as if they had been fragile rose petals beneath a hammer and as she gasped her fingers came up to wind themselves in the tousled thickness of his hair, just the way they used to do.

'V-Vincenzo,' she stumbled out, but the word was blotted out by his kiss—*their* kiss, because her moaned response surely made her a willing participant as she found herself blown away by the power of his touch.

Was it that she was so starved of any kind of adult comfort or pleasure that she found herself submitting to the sweet pleasure of his lips, like a woman drowning in honey? How long since she had been kissed? Not since last time this man had kissed her, and no man had ever kissed her like Vincenzo. No man could. He used his lips to cajole and tease, to tantalise. He made her feel like a woman. A real woman.

Emma moaned as he deepened the kiss in a way designed to have her melting like candle-wax. He knew exactly which buttons to press—he had once told her that he knew her body better than he knew his own—and no one could deny that. But with him it had always been more than technique. It had been helped along with love. At least for a while.

Love.

Mockingly, the word flew into her mind—for where did anything even resembling love feature in this slick seduction of his?

She twisted in his arms. 'Vincenzo...'

Reluctantly, he raised his face from hers, looking down into the dazed dilatation of her eyes—the blue of their rims barely visible, so dark were the pupils which glittered back at him. Her lips were parted, begging to be kissed, and even as he watched the tip of her tiny little pink tongue—which he had tutored to bring him so much pleasure—circled around the parted provocation of her dry lips. She wanted him, he thought with grim satisfaction. She had never stopped wanting him. He moved his hand to rest it with proprietorial carelessness on one knee and felt it tremble. Should he slide it up slowly beneath her dress, to touch her searing heat and make her moan again?

'What is it, Emma?' he asked softly.

'I...I...'

'Do you want me to touch your breast? Your beautiful breast?'

His other hand grazed negligently over an aroused

nipple and it felt as if it were scorching her skin—even though she was covered by her dress—and Emma only just managed to bite back a startled yelp of pleasure. She felt as if she were standing on sensual quicksand—one false step and she would be submerged.

And then she stiffened. Had she imagined the faint buzz of her phone which was buried at the bottom of her handbag? She'd switched it to silent but left it on vibrate—so was she imagining that she could hear it? That her friend was trying desperately to get through to her to tell her that Gino was sick, or crying or just wanted his mummy.

Gino.

She had come here today—spending money she could ill afford on an expensive train ticket—in order to ask her estranged husband for a divorce. So what the hell was she doing in his arms, letting him kiss her, letting her body begin to flower beneath his practised touch? This was a man who *despised* her—he had made that quite plain.

Despite the screaming protest of her senses, she jumped up from the sofa and immediately felt dizzy, but at least she was away from his dangerous intoxication. Hiding her despairing expression, she walked over to the vast window—scarcely noticing the amazing view outside as she leaned back against the glass for support and forced herself to look him in the eye once more.

'Don't do that again, Vincenzo,' she said huskily. 'Don't *ever* do that again!'

'Oh, come *on*, *cara*,' he taunted silkily. 'Never is a long, long time—and you enjoyed that just as much as I did.'

'You…you *forced* yourself on me!' Emma accused, but to her fury he simply laughed.

'If that was force, then I'd love to see you capitulating,' he mocked. 'And please don't play the little innocent with me, because it won't work, not any more,' he warned. 'I know women well enough to know when they are longing to be kissed—and I know you better than most.'

This was *his* territory, she reminded herself—and he was looking dark and predatory and dangerously aroused. He had the upper hand in so many ways—mentally, physically, emotionally and financially—so what was the point in pursuing an argument she wasn't going to win? And did it really matter in the grand scheme of things whether she had surrendered or whether he had manipulated her? In the end it all came down to pride—and she had already decided that pride was a luxury she couldn't afford. So she should forget what had just happened and get down to the important bit.

Yet Emma knew that she was blocking out the most important bit of all. *What about Gino? Now that you can see for yourself that he is the living image of his father—aren't you going to tell Vincenzo that he has a son*? But she was scared—too scared to even want to try. If she told him—who knew what would come of it? Couldn't she just get what she had come for and think about the rest later?

'Are you going to give me a divorce?' she questioned unsteadily.

Silently, he rose to his feet and Emma eyed him as warily as she might have eyed a deadly snake which had just been set loose in the luxurious office. But to her surprise and fury he didn't come anywhere near her, instead went back behind his desk and appeared to check the screen of his computer! As if she had been a brief interlude—already forgotten—and he was now concentrating on far more important things!

'Are you?' she repeated.

'I haven't decided, because, you see, I'm still not sure about your motives for wanting one. And you know me, Emma—I like to have all the available information at my fingertips.' He looked up, his black eyes narrowing thoughtfully. 'You've told me that it isn't because you want to marry another man,' he mused. 'And I believe you.'

'You do?' she questioned, taken aback.

'Sure. Unless you're planning on marrying a eunuch,' he observed sardonically. 'Because you kissed me like a woman who hasn't had sex in a very long time.'

Emma blushed. 'You're disgusting.'

He laughed. 'Since when was sex disgusting? I'm being honest, that's all. So if it isn't a man, then it must be money.' He saw the automatic jerk of her body and knew he'd hit the spot. 'Ah, yes. Of course it is. My guess is that you're broke,' he continued softly. 'You dress like a woman who's broke and you have the general appearance of somebody who hasn't been taking care of herself. So what happened, Emma? Did you forget that you were no longer married to a billionaire but forgot to curb your spending?'

How laughably far from the truth he was—if this was anything to laugh about. And yet he *was* on the right track, wasn't he? He'd accurately judged her to be hard-up—and in Vincenzo's world, money mattered more than anything else. He could *understand* money. He could deal with money in a way he could never deal with emotion.

So why not let him think of her as just some gold-digger who missed the good times? Surely that would throw him off the scent of why she *really* wanted the money. And she knew enough about Vincenzo to realise that he would despise her even more if he thought she was simply inspired by greed. Why, she wouldn't see him again for dust!

'Something like that,' she agreed.

Vincenzo's mouth twisted. So much for all her pretty little denials that she had married him for his money. She had been seduced by his wealth, as he had suspected all along. But in a way, it made dealing with her far simpler.

'Some people might say that you weren't entitled to anything,' he observed.

An arrow of fear ripped through her. 'What are you talking about?'

Vincenzo shrugged. 'We were only married for a

couple of years and there were no children. You're still young, fit, healthy—why should I bankroll the rest of your life simply because I made an error of judgement?'

She flinched. She'd thought that she had reached an emotional-pain threshold, but it seemed she had been wrong. 'I think that a lawyer might see things differently given the disparity in our circumstances,' she said in a low voice. 'As well as the fact that you wouldn't allow me to go out to work, so I'm not exactly number-one choice in the job market.'

'No.' He studied her, at the sudden shaft of harsh winter sunlight which turned her hair into pure, spun gold. 'And just how far are you prepared to go to get a quick divorce?' he questioned softly.

Emma stared at him. *'How far?'* she repeated blankly. 'I don't…I don't quite understand.'

'You don't? Then let me explain it to you so that there can be no possible misunderstanding,' said Vincenzo. 'You want a divorce, while I do not.'

'You—*don't*?' In spite of everything, her foolish heart gave a wild leap and she could barely breathe her next words out. 'May I ask why?'

'Think about it, Emma,' he murmured. 'My marital status makes me unobtainable—and it keeps women off my back.' His eyes glittered. 'Well, in a manner of speaking, you understand.'

Emma froze as his insulting words continued to unfold.

'The moment it becomes known that I'm back on the open market—then I'm going to have to contend with ambitious women, women a little like you once were, who might decide they'd like to be the next Signora Cardini. Who'd like a sexy Sicilian with a big...' his black eyes mocked her; he was enjoying see her wriggle uncomfortably '...bank account,' he finished provocatively as he stretched his arms lazily above his head. 'So you see, in order to grant you a divorce—well, you'd have to make it worth my while, wouldn't you?'

She could feel all the blood drain from her face. But surely he didn't... He couldn't possibly mean what she thought he was hinting at. 'I'm not quite sure what it is you're talking about.'

'Oh, I think you are,' he said softly. 'You want a divorce, and I want you. One last time.'

Emma's fingers crept up to her throat as if that would ease the terrible tension there—for she could barely suck air into her empty lungs. She shook her head, as if she'd misheard him. 'You can't mean that, Vincenzo—'

'But I do. One night with you, Emma. One night of pure and unequivocal sex. To kick over the traces of something which still feels faintly unfinished. One night, that's all.' His black gaze spotlighted her, a smile of unknown origin playing around the corners of his mouth. 'And then I'll give you your divorce.'

There was a long, disbelieving silence as they stared at one another across the vast expanse of the office.

'You...you...you're nothing but a *monster*!' Emma choked out, still not quite believing that this was happening. That the man she had married should be asking her to behave like a...like a woman who would sell her body to the highest bidder!

Vincenzo smiled, feeling the heady rush of pleasure adding to his aching sense of desire as he watched her eyes widen, her face blanch. For this was the woman who had hurt him—who had taken him for a ride, who had hidden the truth from him and ultimately turned her back on him. And he must never forget that, even if she did have the bluest eyes he had ever seen and lips which still begged to be kissed. 'You married me,' he observed caustically. 'You must have known that I had a somewhat...*ruthless* streak. So how about it, Emma? You can't deny that you still want me.'

She shook her head in denial. 'No, I don't.'

His black eyes hardened and so did his groin. 'You little liar,' he drawled. 'But then, lying was always one of your talents.'

She stared at him, flinching from the accusation which was blistering from his black eyes. 'This isn't getting us anywhere. The answer is no. You can go to hell,' she said, grabbing her coat from the back of the chair where she'd left it. 'On second thoughts, hell would be too good a destination for you—they'd probably refuse to let you in!'

He was laughing softly as she headed for the door, watching as she hoisted her handbag over her shoulder, her blonde hair flying wildly behind her, like a pale banner. *'Arrivederci, bella,'* he murmured. 'I'll wait to hear from you.'

Ignoring the startled looks of the glamorous brunette outside his office and the Madonna still sitting at the reception, Emma didn't stop running until she was well away from the building and was certain that nobody was following her. She panted her way to the first bus stop she could find and swallowed down the hot tears which burned at her eyes.

Of all the humiliating propositions he could have put to her—that topped the list. The man was a monster—a *monster*! Stepping onto the lumbering double-decker bus, she pulled out her cell phone, but thankfully the screen remained blank. At least there had been no emergency calls from Joanna, which meant that Gino must be all right. And they weren't expecting her back until much later.

The large red bus moved slowly along in the bus lane and normally Emma might have admired the glittering circle of the London Eye, which looked so futuristic compared to the ancient Houses of Westminster—but she could see nothing. Feel nothing. Her mind and her body felt numb—as if what had just happened had been like a horrible dream.

An outsider might have urged her to play her biggest card of all—and to tell the proud Sicilian that he was now a father. But some bone-deep fear stopped her—the very real fear that he would step in to take over or, even worse, try to take Gino away from her. And given his power and his wealth—when measured up against her lack of skills and poverty—wouldn't he stand a chance of being able to do just that?

Emma shook her head as she put her travel card back inside her purse. She couldn't tell him—how *could* she? And even if she did, he wouldn't believe her—for hadn't it been her supposed infertility which had driven the last terrible wedge between them and finally ended their unhappy marriage?

She clamped her eyes closed and bit her lip to try to keep the memories at bay, but that didn't seem to work. Her mind had ideas of its own and it took her back—right back—to a time before all the acrimony and bitterness.

A time when Vincenzo had loved her.

CHAPTER FOUR

EMMA had met Vincenzo when she was coming out of a vulnerable period of her life—not long after the death of her mother, Edie. Edie's illness had been sudden and Emma had dropped out of catering college to care for the woman who had given birth to her. She'd done it out of love and, yes, out of a certain sense of duty—but also because there was no one else to do it.

But Edie had fought her prognosis every bit of the way. The disease had dragged on and on and those final months had been spent in pursuit of an impossible cure. The slightest hint of any new treatment would be enough for the instant signing of cheques. Edie had gone to faith-healers and psychics. She had eaten nothing but apricots and drunk nothing but warm water for a week. She had undergone ice-therapy in an exclusive Swiss spa but nothing had made any difference; nothing could have done.

It had been a miserable time culminating in an angry death, and afterwards Emma had been left feeling empty, unwilling to go back to life at catering college, which she had seemed to have grown out of. Almost as an antidote to grief, she had taken a job in a shop while Edie's affairs were sorted out and the lawyers worked out how much money remained.

And that was when Emma had discovered that there was virtually nothing left. Huge debts had been run up to support all the alternative treatment—the family house had needed to be sold and after all the bills had been paid there had been nothing more than a few hundred pounds in the kitty.

Uncharacteristically, Emma had decided to blow the money. She'd seen too much sadness to want to plan for a future which no one could guarantee—and such a small amount could give her nothing in the way of security anyway. Life had suddenly seemed too short to measure out a cup of sultanas. She'd wanted sun and history and beauty of the harsh and uncompromising kind, so she had gone to Sicily.

And met Vincenzo.

It was one of those days which would for ever be etched on her mind in rich and vibrant colours. A rare break from her cultural tour of the island, and it found her on a stunning beach with her hat and her book, letting the warmth of the sun soak into her pale skin.

She was very aware that her blonde, English looks excited attention wherever she went and took care to cover her head and shoulders when she visited churches and cathedrals, as local custom demanded. Her dresses

were always knee-length and her make-up kept so light
as to be almost non-existent.

But on the day she discovered a deserted little cove
not far from where she was staying, she gave in to what
she had been longing to do. She peeled off her dress to
reveal a sleek one-piece swimsuit and began splashing
in the water as the dark cares of the last months were
gradually washed away.

Afterwards she must have fallen asleep, because she
awoke to see a shadow falling over her and a man standing looking down at her. He was dark and lean and
muscular, his black hair ruffled by the faint breeze
which blew in off the sea. But she had noticed him
before—who wouldn't? She remembered seeing him
while drinking her morning coffee in the square and he
had zipped past on one of the little scooters which all
the Sicilian men seemed to ride.

Up close, he was even more amazing—and he was
looking at her now with a lazy and yet blatant sexual
scrutiny. Maybe she should have been frightened, and
on one level perhaps she was—but on another…

Something in his black eyes and faintly cruel lips
cried out to some deep, elemental core which she hadn't
believed existed—certainly not in her. Because Emma
was a dreamer, a reader—and she had never met anyone
who could match the romantic and physical impact of
the characters she read about in novels.

Until now.

He was wearing a pair of faded jeans and an

equally faded T-shirt and his bare toes dug into the soft, silvery sand.

'*Come si chiama?*' he questioned softly.

It seemed crazy—rude—not to give him an answer, and impossible, too, when those ebony eyes were searing into her and demanding one. 'Emma. Emma Shreve.'

'Ah, you understand Italian?'

She shook her head, telling herself that she shouldn't be striking up a conversation with a total stranger, but feeling carefree for the first time in ages. 'Not really, but I try—I'm not one of those people who go somewhere expecting that everyone should speak *my* language. And Italian's not too bad.' She sighed. 'It's Sicilian which is the killer.'

She hadn't known it at the time but it was exactly the right thing to say to a fiercely proud Sicilian. 'And what is *your* name?' she questioned politely.

'It's Vincenzo. Vincenzo Cardini,' he replied, watching her carefully.

It was to be a while before Emma was to learn about the far-reaching influence and power of the Cardini family. That day she assumed he was just a regular guy—though one with extraordinary charisma which seemed to sizzle off him in a searing dark heat. He sat down beside her and shared her water. He made her laugh. And when the sun was too hot, he took her for lunch in a luscious restaurant and bought her *sarde a beccafico*—the most delicious meal she'd ever eaten, and a dish whose complexity she would later learn displayed great wealth.

He spoke of the island of his birth with a passion and a knowledge which made all her guidebooks seem sorely lacking. He sighed when he told her that he came here only on vacation these days, and that his business was based mainly in Rome. She asked him lots of intelligent questions about his work, mainly to try to focus on something other than the rugged beauty of his face.

But when he tried to kiss her before they parted, she stopped him with a shake of her blonde hair.

'Sorry, I don't kiss strangers.'

He smiled a lazy smile. 'And I don't take no for an answer.'

'This time you do,' said Emma, but she wouldn't have been human if she hadn't been regretful as he put her fingertips to his lips instead and captured her eyes in a stare which made her feel weak.

Uninvited, he called at the small hotel where she was staying and naturally she agreed to see him again. How could she not, when already she was halfway in love with him, and he with her? A *colpo di fulmine*, he called it—but with the air of a man who had been visited by something unwelcome. A thunderbolt, he said darkly.

By day he showed her his island home—though he kept her away from any of his family. His own parents were dead, he had been reared by his grandmother and had hundreds of Cardini cousins who 'would not approve of us seeing one another, *cara*,' he told her lazily.

But what did she care about that when each night he took her a little further towards a pleasure she could not have dreamed existed? She had wondered if he might think her a clumsy innocent, but Vincenzo seemed to enjoy tutoring her as much as he enjoyed her instinctive restraint. He told her that it proved she was not easy, as so many of her compatriots were. The girls who came to Sicily looking for a dark and proficient lover and gave their bodies as casually as they gave their orders at the bars.

Everything seemed perfect until the night she at last allowed him to share her bed and the see-sawing of terrible emotions which followed their lovemaking. Pain, disbelief, joy—and then, finally, a red-hot kind of anger as he sat up in bed and stared at her as if he had been visited by a spectre.

'Why didn't you tell me?' he roared.

Emma shrank back against the rumpled sheets. 'I didn't know how to!'

'You didn't know how to?' he repeated. His voice was bitter. 'And so you have allowed *this* to happen.' He shook his dark head. 'I have robbed you of your virginity—the most precious thing that a woman possesses.'

But by next morning his rage had abated and in those next last few days he taught her how to love her body—and his. So that when he came to the airport to say goodbye, Emma wept for all that she had found and now would lose for ever.

She didn't expect to hear from him again, but unexpectedly he turned up in England—telling her furiously that he couldn't get her out of his mind, as if she had

committed some kind of crime for being the cause of
his obsession. When he discovered that she had no ties
nor permanent job, he took her back with him to
Rome—where she realised that she was actually dating
a fabulously wealthy man.

Installing her in his luxury apartment as his mistress,
he bought her a brand-new wardrobe, dressing her up
as if she were a doll and transforming her into a woman
who turned heads. Emma blossomed beneath his atten-
tions, though she was slightly shocked to discover that
her transformation had unleashed a terrible kind of
jealousy. He suspected even his friends of coveting her.

'You know that they want you?' he demanded.

'I can assure you that the feeling isn't reciprocated.'

'I cannot bear the thought of another man having
you!' he raged. 'Not now—and not ever!'

Was it to possess her utterly and completely that he
married her—or was it simply because he felt that he
had compromised himself by robbing her of her inno-
cence? But marriage also meant acceptability from his
family in Sicily, and provided the respectable arena for
something else Vincenzo wanted more than all the
wealth in the universe.

'A son,' he breathed on their wedding night as he
stroked her flat, bare belly and moved over her with dark
intent. 'I will put my son inside your body, Emma.'

Who wouldn't have thrilled at that avowal? Certainly
not a woman swept up in the dizzy whirl of love. But
the tenor of their lovemaking seemed to change from

that very moment. There seemed to be a *purpose* to it which had not been there before. And the inevitable disappointment each month when his longed-for son failed to materialise made Emma begin to get twitchy.

On one of their periodic visits to Sicily, even his favourite cousin Salvatore, who clearly still disapproved of her—marriage or no marriage—was heard to allude to babies. Or, rather, the lack of them. Emma felt both insulted, and hurt.

Soon the subject began to dominate their thoughts, if not their conversation—for Vincenzo flatly refused to discuss it—and, driven to despair, Emma went secretly to see an English doctor on the Via Martinotti in Rome.

The news was devastating enough, but Emma was frightened into stuffing the letter into a drawer, supposedly to disclose to Vincenzo when she found the 'right' time—though quite when she imagined that time might be always perplexed her afterwards. For how did you find the words to tell a man that his greatest wish was destined never to be fulfilled?

Vincenzo found the letter. Was waiting for her one afternoon with it crumpled in his hand, his face dark, an expression in his eyes she had never seen there before and which sent shivers of foreboding icing over her skin.

'When were you going to tell me?' he questioned, in a voice which sounded flat and unfamiliar. 'Or perhaps you weren't going to bother?'

'Of course I was!'

'When?'

'When the time seemed right,' Emma answered miserably.

'And when would that be? Is there an optimum time for announcing to your husband that you are unable to have his child?'

Emma bit her lip. 'We can investigate fertility treatment…*adopt*,' she ventured, but there was no answering light of hope in the stony black eyes. 'Or I can see another specialist for a second opinion.'

'If you say so.'

She had never seen Vincenzo like this before, like a tyre which had been lanced by a shard of glass—all the air and the life seemed to have left him.

Her infertility drove a further wedge between them— that was as clear as the stars in the night sky—but Vincenzo preferred to focus instead on her deceit. The fact that she had gone to the doctor *in secret*. That she had kept the fact *hidden* from him. Until one day Emma realised that, no matter how much she tried to explain or justify her reasons, he *needed* someone to blame, and who better than her? He had swum against the tide by marrying an English girl instead of a Sicilian one— but he had made a bad choice and chosen one who was barren, too.

It became one of those simple if heartbreaking decisions. Was she going to allow their marriage to wither away completely in front of her eyes, destroying even the few good memories left—or was she strong and brave enough to give Vincenzo his freedom by walking away?

He didn't fight her when she told him she was leaving—though his face became as hard and as forbidding as some dark stone. He probably wouldn't even notice when she was gone, she thought bitterly—for wasn't he just spending longer and longer days at the office, sometimes not even bothering to come home in time for dinner?

The icy chill which greeted her decision lasted until she reached the door, and then she turned to say goodbye for the last time, something in his eyes stopped her.

'Vincenzo?' she said, hesitantly.

And then he started to kiss her—and all the sadness and bitterness and lost love bubbled up and spilled over as he drove into her up against the wall by the front door. He made her miss her plane and then carried her upstairs one last time for one long night of exquisitely heartbreaking sex.

She opened her eyes as he was getting dressed and that was when his face grew hard and cold and he said it: 'Get out of here, Emma, and do not come back—for you are no wife of mine.' And then he turned away, and walked out of the room.

Later that morning her plane had taken off and she had been blinded by tears.

And about a month later had discovered she was pregnant....

'Next stop Waterloo!' The bus driver's voice broke into Emma's reverie and with a start she realised that the bus was slowing down outside the railway station. And that nothing had been resolved.

Like a woman walking in her sleep, she got off the bus and went into the station concourse to find a coffee shop, barely noticing the crowds of people milling around. It felt strange to be out on her own without a little baby in her care. How peculiar to just be able to walk up to a table and sit down without having to negotiate a buggy, or worry that he wouldn't want to sit still.

She stared at the creamy mounds of foam on her cappuccino as the dull feeling of disquiet refused to leave her—and it went much deeper than just the worry of how she was going to survive. No, her uneasiness had been provoked by seeing Vincenzo again—and no longer being able to deny the glaring truth.

That Gino was his living image!

Pulling her little photo wallet out of her bag, she stared down at the most recent snap of him and the sight of his gorgeous little face made her heart clench with pain and guilt. Had she been deliberately blocking out just how like his father he was? As a safety mechanism to protect her own broken heart, without thinking of *their* needs?

At that moment, the phone began to ring and she grabbed it. An unknown number. Yet Emma knew exactly who it was.

Heart pounding, she clicked the connection with a trembling finger. 'Hello?'

'Have you thought any more about my offer, *cara*?'

And suddenly Emma knew that she couldn't keep running away—because she had reached a dead end and there was nowhere left to run. And neither could she keep the truth from her estranged husband any longer. He needed to know about Gino and she needed to tell him.

'Yes,' she said slowly. 'I've thought about nothing else. I need to see you.' And why not get it over with? What would be the point of having to arrange another day of babysitting when she was already here in the capital? 'I can meet you later, after all.'

So she had changed her mind, as he had known she would. In one lustful rush, Vincenzo experienced triumph, anticipation, and yet it was accompanied by a bitter kind of disappointment, too. For hadn't he admired the feisty way she'd thrown his admittedly insulting offer back in his face? Hadn't there been echoes in that of the woman he'd fallen in love with—the one who had shown restraint, who had refused to tumble into bed with him just because he had wanted her to?

But no. It seemed that he had been right all along, and that everyone had their price—even Emma. His mouth hardened. *Especially* Emma.

'I'm tied up with meetings all afternoon. Do you know the Vinoly Hotel?' he questioned coolly.

'I've heard of it.'

'Meet me there at six—in the Bay Room bar.'

Emma closed her eyes with relief. A public place. She could tell him there and that was the best possible option—for surely even Vincenzo wouldn't lose his rag in the middle of some fancy hotel. 'I'll be there.'

'*Ciao*,' said Vincenzo in a silky voice as he replaced the phone.

Emma dug her fingernails into the palms of her hands. She was going to have to ring Joanna and tell her she'd be later than planned and then she was going to have to find some way of occupying herself for the afternoon. To work out the best way to tell him that he had a child. She dreaded to think what Vincenzo's reaction would be—but, no matter what he threw at her, she must face it. She must be strong and take it. For her own sake—but, more especially, for Gino's.

vanished to her feet, and Emma swallowed, a faint flicker
of unease in her stomach as she recognised the quite
different style and class of what she was used to—like
champagne compared to a glass of water. Another sip,
another mouthful.

CHAPTER FIVE

EMMA spent the afternoon walking aimlessly around
the city and ended up window-shopping in the glitziest
department store she could find, taking advantage of one
of the rest rooms to wash her hands and fringe and apply
a lick of make-up.

Vincenzo's comments of earlier had made her feel
scrawny and unattractive—and that was the last thing she
needed as she was about to walk into one of the capital's
smartest hotels and drop this particular bombshell.

Her heart was thundering as she walked into the Bay
Room bar and she could see Vincenzo standing talking
to a member of staff—looking tall and eye-catching in
his dark suit, and totally at home in this upmarket venue.

Nervously, she glanced around. Seated at the trade-
mark triangular tables with their distinctive turquoise
velvet seats were the movers and shakers of the city.
Women wearing amazing sleek and expensive clothes
and gravity-defying high-heeled shoes.

And, despite her newly washed fringe and the liberal

amount of scent and hand lotion with which she'd doused herself in the rest room, Emma had never felt quite so out of place in her life. She felt like one of those characters from a Victorian novel—a scruffy little urchin who'd taken a break from selling matches on a street corner outside—and if there had been a choice, she would have turned around and walked straight out. But she didn't have a choice, not any more.

Vincenzo watched her walk in, his black eyes giving nothing away as they flicked over her in brief assessment. So she hadn't spent the afternoon buying herself something new to wear, he noted—as most women who were planning to sleep with a man again would do. Which must mean that she really *was* broke—or that she was still very confident about her sexual allure over him. His mouth twisted. Or both.

'*Ciao*, Emma,' he murmured as she approached.

'Hello,' she said, feeling ridiculously self-conscious, aware of the bizarreness of the situation and the fact that the member of staff was looking at her as if some alien had just dropped in through the ceiling.

'The *maître d'* has just been telling me that, unfortunately, all the tables are taken,' Vincenzo was saying smoothly. 'But that he has arranged drinks for us on the rooftop terrace.'

'You will find the view from the terrace infinitely superior sir,' said the *maître d'* with the affable smile of a man who had just been handed a large wad of money. 'I will have someone accompany you to the penthouse.'

He snapped his fingers and a man in uniform who looked about twelve began to lead the way towards one of the lifts.

Emma's eyes told Vincenzo that she didn't believe a word of it and the mockery in his black eyes told her that he didn't care. But how could she possibly object with a third party present—and had he been banking on that? Or was it just that he was aware of his bargaining power and that she must play to his rules if she wanted her divorce settlement?

The silence was suffocating as the lift rode upwards and it seemed to grow more and more oppressive as the bell-boy showed them into what was clearly a very large suite of rooms dominated by a vast sitting room studded with dramatic arrangements of flowers. It was true that the view was magnificent—a floor-to-ceiling firework display of glittering stars and skyscrapers against the indigo backdrop of the sky. But more glaringly obvious was a set of double doors which led through to a room dominated by the biggest bed she had ever seen. Emma bit her lip. It was an insult—a blatant and glaring insult.

'Will there be anything else, sir?'

'No, that will be all, thanks.'

She waited until the boy had shut the doors behind him before turning on Vincenzo, who was taking his jacket off. 'You said a drink. This is a suite!' she accused.

Vincenzo smiled as he loosened his tie. So she wanted to play games, did she? 'The two aren't mutually incompatible, surely?' With a careless hand, he indicated the ice-bucket containing champagne. 'Drink all you like, *cara*.'

'Are you saying that a table wouldn't magically have become available if you'd asked for one?' Emma asked, wishing she could rid herself of the terrible nerves which were criss-crossing through her stomach and beginning to tie it up in knots.

'I could have asked for one,' he conceded. 'But you cannot deny that up here it is so much more comfortable—and so much more private, of course.' He poured out champagne, which fizzed up like pale gold into two tall flutes, his eyes glittering with insolent challenge—wondering how long she was going to carry on playing the innocent. 'Take off your coat and lets have a drink. You said you had something you wanted to tell me.'

Nerves had suddenly clutched at her throat as if someone had placed their hands there and were squeezing all the breath from her body. Emma nodded, slipped her coat off, perched on the edge of the sofa and took the drink from him, although she noticed that he didn't pick up a glass himself.

It had been a long time since she'd drunk champagne and its sudden heady rush reminded her that she hadn't eaten anything since breakfast. She felt dizzy. Weakened by his proximity and the way that he was looking at her. *So tell him.*

'Vincenzo…this is very difficult.'

He sat down beside her. He could see her trembling

and his lips curved into an arrogant smile. Had an earlier taste of his kisses reminded her just what she'd been missing? She really *did* want him. 'Is it?' he questioned, with soft arrogance.

Taking the half-drunk glass from her unprotesting fingers and putting it down on a table, he ran a thoughtful finger along the too-severe jut of her collar-bone, feeling her shiver beneath his touch. 'It's only difficult if we make it so. If you try and dress it up to be something it isn't. Why not just admit that we're still physically attracted to one another and that we both want this?'

Emma stared at him in rapidly escalating horror. He thought…he really *did* think she'd come back to strike the deal—a quick divorce in exchange for a night of sex. 'That wasn't what I meant.'

But Vincenzo wasn't listening. He was hungry for her, transfixed by the way her rapid breathing was making her breasts rise and fall—and he was feeling more fired up than he could remember feeling since that last time he'd made love to her. His mouth hardened. Or, rather, had *sex* with her. There had been no love involved in that last frantic coming together that day in Rome. Maybe there never had been. Maybe thunderbolts were merely the indiscriminate strikings of lust.

'I don't care,' he said deliberately. 'In fact, I don't care about anything—only this.'

His mouth came down on hers—a slow, drugging kiss with all the passion he'd displayed earlier in his offices, but this time there was a difference. This time they were not on *his* territory with the possibility that his assistant might wiggle her way in at any moment. And this time Emma knew that she was beaten—in every way. In a few minutes' time she was going to tell Vincenzo something which would change his life irrevocably.

She was going to have to learn to live with his anger and the contempt she knew deep down that he was keeping on ice because at this moment he wanted her. And didn't she want him, too? If she was being honest, then she had never really stopped wanting him. So why couldn't she have this one last time before all the recriminations started? One last taste of bliss before the dark clouds descended.

'Vincenzo,' she groaned as she reached up to cling onto his broad shoulders and felt their muscular power. 'Oh, *Vincenzo.*'

He closed his mind to the memories stirred up by her breathless words, instead pulling her closer into his arms, feeling her petite frame trembling beneath his touch and the soft, silken spill of her hair as it brushed against his cheek. The fierce throbbing at his groin was setting him on fire, and he kissed her more thoroughly than he could ever remember kissing anyone before—his lips exploring hers as if he couldn't bear to tear his mouth away. What *was* it that she did to him?

'Touch me!' he urged huskily. 'Touch me the way you used to.'

The faint sense of vulnerability in his deep voice was almost too much to bear—as intoxicating as his shuddered entreaty—or was Emma just imagining that? Hearing what she wanted to hear. But either way, she was in too deep to want to do anything other than what he wanted—and she ran her hands luxuriously down over his chest, feeling the roughness of hair beneath the fine silk of his shirt.

'Like that?' she whispered.

'Piu!'

'More?'

'*Sì*! More. Much more.'

Her fingers whispered down to his groin, where he was unashamedly aroused, and he bit out a remark which sounded like some Sicilian curse, and she thought that it probably was. As if he despised being in thrall to his senses like this, even while his body revelled in it. 'Like this?'

'*Sì*, exactly like that. Ah, Emma,' he groaned. Pale witch of a woman! Experimentally, he ran his hands over her body—this body he knew so well—as if he were feeling it for the first time. And maybe he was. He frowned. It felt different. Not only a diminishment of flesh, but her breasts seemed to be a different shape, too—or at least as much as he could tell while she was still covered up. He cupped one and let his thumb graze across it.

'Take this damned dress off,' he instructed.

But even in the midst of her body's heated clamour, Emma was assailed by nerves. Surely he wasn't expecting her to leap up and start stripping off for him—the way she might once have done when they were newly married? In view of their situation wouldn't that be impossible? Why, she would feel as if he was buying her. *And isn't he?* jeered the mocking voice of her conscience. *Isn't he?*

But Emma closed her ears and her mind to the uncomfortable taunt and licked her dry lips. 'You…you take it off.'

'If you insist,' he murmured.

He was good at that, of course. He must have removed a million dresses in his time. And how many other women had he undressed since the last time she'd been in his arms? wondered Emma painfully as he peeled the cheap little garment from her body, letting it fall disdainfully to the floor.

As he moved away from her his black eyes scorched over her like a diabolical laser beam. 'Let me look at you.'

She wanted to shrink her arms over her chest and bunch her knees up to hide from the inevitable critical assessment of her scrawny body and her plain underwear, and her…

'Tights!' he bit out derisively. 'Since when did you start wearing tights?'

Since she stopped being a billionaire's possession, that was when. Maybe her estranged husband didn't realise that sliding into silk stockings and suspender belt wasn't exactly compatible with getting up at the crack of dawn to feed a baby.

The thought of the baby and what she was going to have to tell Vincenzo was enough to make Emma freeze momentarily—to want to call a halt to it and tell him that this was a fruitless exercise. But by now he was tugging the tights down over her ankles and off her toes and burying his head into the apex of her thighs—kissing her there, over her plain cotton panties, until she was wriggling impatiently, wanting him with a fierce desire which was almost unbearable.

'Vincenzo,' she gasped.

'You want to go to bed?' he demanded hotly.

And break the mood? Giving her time for second thoughts? Allowing reason to creep in and ruin something that was making her feel more alive than she had done in so long? Her head said this was probably one of the craziest things she had ever done but her body had other ideas. And he was still her husband, Emma thought achingly—surely this was her *right* as much as her pleasure.

'No,' she whispered, tangling her fingers in the ebony waves of his hair, the way she'd done innumerable times before. 'Let's do it here.'

Vincenzo groaned at her easy capitulation—at her effortless transformation from ice queen to siren. But he had always loved the fiery passion which lay beneath the cool blonde exterior. That streak of sensual unconventionality he had coaxed from her—at least until those last glacial months of the marriage. He had taught her everything she knew—why should he not taste the fruits of his labour one more time, to see if she had improved during his absence from her bed? 'Take off my shirt,' he gritted out.

Her trembling fingers struggled to slide the delicate fabric over the infinitely silkier surface of his skin, her fingers gently clawing in little circles at the whorls of hair which grew there, but he stilled them with the flat of his hand. 'Later,' he said unsteadily. 'There will be time for that later—but for now…'

He was pulling at the buckle of his belt and Emma was thinking that *there would be no later*—a certain knowledge told her that even while her nagging conscience urged her to tell him. Tell him *now*. But she did not heed it—she could not—for a broken little sound was torn from her throat as she touched her lips greedily to his shoulders and his neck. Her lips brushed against the rough rasp of his jaw, grazing softly along its proud, curved line, and she heard his ragged sigh of pleasure.

How cruel sex could be, she thought, with a shiver. And not just cruel, but clever, too—because it could make you feel things which weren't real. It could make you believe that you still loved someone…and she didn't love Vincenzo—of course she didn't. How could she possibly love him after everything that had happened?

She watched as he moved away to remove the last of his clothing and then pushed her back against the sofa as he came to her—with a dark, sexual power she had almost forgotten. For a moment time was frozen as he towered over her like some dark and golden colossus before he slid down onto her waiting skin.

'Vincenzo!' she gasped as he entered her with one long and delicious thrust, filling her completely. For a moment he stilled and looked down at her, his black eyes opaque with lust and a fleeting glimpse of something else, too—something which looked like anger. But surely not anger at a time like this? 'Vincenzo?' she said again, only this time on a question.

He shook his head slightly as he began to move within her, despising her sexual power over him even as he felt it rip his senses apart with such an overload of sensual delight. He stared down at the vision she made beneath him—her eyes tightly closed and her cheeks growing pink as she lifted those perfect legs and wrapped them tightly around his back.

And hadn't doing this to her haunted his dreams for too long? Surely this would rid him of her pervasive spell once and for all. His mouth hardened. 'Look at me,' he ordered softly. 'Look at me, Emma.'

Reluctantly, she allowed her eyelids to flutter open. When your eyes were closed you could imagine. Invent. Pretend that this was happening for no other reason than that two people loved one another. How far from the truth that was—how complex the motives which had brought both of them here, to this place. She stared up into the taut tension of his face. 'Oh, Vincenzo,' she whispered.

'Oh, Vincenzo!' he mocked as he curled the palms of his hands underneath her bare buttocks. 'Am I the best lover you've ever had, Emma?'

'You…you know you are!' she gasped out, aware that he wanted to hurt her—but suddenly she was past caring, for he had brought her to that point where it was all

going to happen, and far sooner than she had thought.
As if he were catapulting her up to the stars and then
bringing her down again in slow and delicious motion.
'Vincenzo…oh, *oh!* Oh…*yes*…yes…*ye-e-s-s*!'

He felt her body clenching around him and forced
himself to hold back for just long enough to watch her
wild abandon as her head fell back and her nails dug into
his shoulders. And then he let go and took his own
pleasure and he could never remember it washing over
him with such strength—making him completely powerless in its wake. It seemed to go on and on as if it were
never going to stop—and even after it was over and had
subsided he stayed inside her for a moment while the
final spasms ebbed away.

He looked down at her flushed face, at the strand of
hair which clung to one damp cheek. In the past he
might have pushed that strand away and curled it around
his finger, but not now—for such a gesture would imply
some kind of tenderness, and tenderness was the last
thing he was feeling.

He pulled out of her and moved away, getting up
from the sofa and walking over to pour himself a glass
of water, lifting it to his lips and drinking from it, his
black eyes capturing her gaze over its rim. 'Do you realise that we were so *up for it*—as you might say—that
we failed to consider contraception?' he mocked. 'But,
as we both know, that is not a subject which needs trouble us.'

Disbelievingly, Emma stared across the room at him,

trembling now. How unimaginably *cruel*. Had he saved the most wounding barb of all for last—to say something as confrontational as that, after they had just shared the greatest intimacy of all? To try to cold-bloodedly hurt her as nothing else could? Well, he was wrong—as he was about to discover—but wasn't his brutality at such a moment a timely reminder not to weave any foolish fantasies about Vincenzo Cardini?

'That remark was completely unnecessary,' she said stiffly.

'Was it?' he mocked. 'But it's the truth.'

Surely he was never going to believe her when she told him how very wrong he was? Emma reached for her bra and pants. She was going to have to tell him, but she was damned if she was going to be naked when she did so.

He watched her getting dressed but was disinclined to stop her. If he wanted her again then he would simply undress her quickly—but right now all he felt was distaste. How quickly the urges of the body could mask the reality of a situation, he thought—and once passion had been spent all you were left with were the cold, hard facts.

Emma was nothing to him now other than a duplicitous wife who had just submitted to sex in order to secure a speedy divorce deal! He began to pull his own clothes on, eager now to be away from her.

'Vincenzo.' Emma finished pulling her dress down over her head and pushing her disarrayed hair back from her flushed face before turning to face him. 'You remember I said that I had something to tell you.'

He barely flicked her a glance as he finished buttoning his shirt and slipped his shoes on. 'I can hardly wait,' he said sarcastically.

She drew a deep breath. How many ways were there to say it? Only one—because the words were so powerful that nothing, *nothing* was ever going to be able to lessen their irrevocable impact. But how could she tell him—how *could* she?

'Vincenzo. You've got...I mean...we've got...' Emma cleared her throat, aware of the furious, frightened hammering of her heart. 'The thing is, you see—we have a son. A son. You have a son.'

CHAPTER SIX

FOR a moment Vincenzo thought that he must have misheard her, though something in the strangled quality of Emma's tone alerted his senses to something far more complicated than a mere misunderstanding. Narrowing his eyes into disbelieving shards, he stared at her. '*What* did you say?' he questioned menacingly.

Emma swallowed. 'You've…you've got a son, Vincenzo. Or, rather, *we've* got a son. His name is—'

'Shut up—just shut up!' he bit out in disgust, his words silencing her and his hands clenching into fists by the powerful shafts of his thighs, caught up in the grip of a rage fiercer than anything he could remember. For a moment he wanted to storm across the room and shake her, but he didn't trust himself. His mouth twisted into a cruel curve of contempt. 'You can have your damned divorce, Emma—after all, you've just earned it. The sex was laughably brief, but as a cathartic measure it was probably worth it—just please don't spin me any more of your damned lies.'

Emma shook her head, blocking out his insults and trying to focus solely on the truth. 'But it isn't a lie—I swear, it isn't.'

'You *swear* it?' His eyes were blazing black fire. 'How do you dare claim such a thing to me in view of our history?' he demanded, his mind spinning as he tried to pluck facts from her unbelievable statement. And one fact leapt out from all the others. He frowned. 'You say you have a child?'

'Yes.'

'But that is not possible.' He took an unwise step closer, his voice tight with gritted fury. 'You are infertile, Emma. You can't have children. The doctor told you so in one of your private consultations. He sent you a letter stating just that, which I still have in my possession. Surely you haven't forgotten that?'

'Of course I haven't forgotten—'

'Then how in hell's name can you have a baby, and how can I possibly be the father?' he roared.

Emma swallowed. 'Can we please talk about this calmly?'

'*Calmly?*' Vincenzo's voice was like black ice. 'Are you out of your mind? You drop a lie—'

'It's not a lie!' she repeated desperately. 'Why the hell would I lie to you about something like that?'

'I can think of a pretty good reason,' he retorted sourly. 'Missing my wealth and deciding you want a sizeable chunk of it might be enough to make you go ahead with some kind of scam—'

'*Scam?*' she echoed in horror. 'You think I'm some kind of...some kind of...cheap *con-merchant*?'

He shrugged, his heart pounding furiously in his chest. 'You've already proved that, Emma. You fooled me into believing that we were still trying for a baby, when all the time you knew that it was impossible. If that isn't conning someone, then I'd be interested to hear your definition of the word, *cara*.'

Never had a term of supposed affection carried with it such a wealth of withering scorn, and Emma almost recoiled from the look of disdain which sparked from his black eyes. Her tongue snaked around lips which suddenly felt like crumpled parchment. 'I never meant to deceive you,' she whispered.

'No?'

'I was frightened to let you know what the results were,' she said.

'So you treated me like a fool!' he accused. 'You just thought you'd keep me in the dark about something as important as that?'

'No. Of course not. It wasn't meant to be like that. I *was* going to tell you—'

'And what precisely *were* you going to tell me, Emma?' he questioned in a suddenly silken voice.

Emma relaxed a little. 'That I couldn't...couldn't have a baby.'

'Yet now you are telling me that the doctor was wrong? That all those months of trying vainly to conceive were an illusion—and that you *could* conceive after all?'

'Yes! My obstetrician said that these things do happen occasionally—'

'Miraculous,' he commented sarcastically. 'And when did this marvel occur? How old is the child?'

A part of her wanted to tell him to forget it—that she wasn't going to *beg* him to acknowledge his son, and that she had more than enough love to go round.

But Emma recognised that she must do this for Gino's sake. Because what if one day he turned round and demanded to know where his father was? She must be able to look him in the eye and tell him truthfully that she had told Vincenzo everything—every single fact— even if she'd told them to him rather late in the day. How Vincenzo chose to interpret and then act on those facts was up to him, but her conscience would be clear.

'He's ten months old,' she said—knowing that this was the big one and watching while Vincenzo's eyes narrowed in silent calculation. He was clearly doing some kind of rapid mathematical assessment about whether or not it was possible for him to be the father. And, yes, it was insulting, but her feelings were not the issue here.

'And when are you claiming that this conception took place?'

'It must have been that…that last time we were together. Do you remember?'

Now he gave a grim kind of smile. 'Do I remember? I am hardly likely to forget,' he said bitterly. It had been the first time they'd been together for weeks. Their relationship had gradually been eroding, but in the light of the news that she could not bear his child and all the accompanying deceit they had become strangers to one another. The letter she had hidden had become the symbol of all that was wrong between them. He began to doubt whether *anything* about her had been genuine.

'So were you really a virgin when I met you, Emma?' he had demanded icily one day, over breakfast. 'Or was that, too, a fabrication?'

He remembered the way that the light had gone out of her eyes and, yes, he had taken pleasure in that, too.

'Oh, what is the point, Vincenzo?' had been her dull response. 'If you can think so poorly of me, then there is no point in going on, is there?'

He remembered the feeling of relief which had washed over him, telling himself that he would be glad to see the back of her lying little face. True, he would have to live with the mockery of his cousins, who had always cautioned him against the marriage—but he could deal with that.

Yet the reality of their separation had proved harsher than he had anticipated. He had missed her bright blonde hair and her sunny smile and the way that her delicate frame used to complement his own powerful body so perfectly. Until he reminded himself that those were external things which were easily replaceable and that, in truth, he didn't really recognise the Emma he had married. His trust in her had been destroyed—and to a proud Sicilian man trust was everything.

He was aware of the bizarre situation in which he now found himself—aware of Emma standing wide-eyed on the opposite side of the luxury hotel suite, her cheeks still flushed from their lovemaking and her hair in disarray. So what was he going to do about her extraordinary revelation that he had fathered her child?

Giving himself time to sift through his options with a chilly detachment, which his business rivals would have recognised with sinking hearts, Vincenzo poured himself another glass of mineral water and drank from it. For once, he could have done with the slightly numbing effect of alcohol, but he needed his wits to be as razor sharp as they had ever been.

His black gaze bored into her like the twin barrels of a shotgun. 'The question is—whether or not I believe you,' he pondered. 'Or whether you're just spinning me a line to try to get your hands on as much of my money as possible.'

Emma choked back her instinctive gasp of distress. 'You think that I'd choose this particular method as a means of extorting money from a man like you? That I'd put myself through all this grief?' she demanded. 'Why, I'd rather scrub floors to earn a crust than do that!'

'So why don't you?' he challenged icily.

His words were the final straw—pushing her and pushing her until all her determination to stay calm flew out of the window and something inside Emma snapped. All the worry and the struggle of the preceding months, the huge decision to tell Vincenzo and then her own weakness in having just had sex with him—all these factors now ignited to explode into a debilitating cocktail of anger and indignation and sheer anxiety.

'Because I have a baby to look after and it's actually very difficult, if you must know! I'd pay more in childcare than I'd earn! But how would you know—when you've been cushioned by wealth all your life? Everything you've wanted has always been there for the taking. Money may have made your life easier, Vincenzo, but it has tarnished it, too, because you are unable to see anything except through its dark and corrupting influence. Every time you meet a new person the barriers go up and you're thinking, *Does this person want to know me, or do they want to get their hands on my millions?*'

'That's *enough*!' he snapped. 'I don't really think that you are in a position to give me a lecture on the morality of money, when your own morals are in radical need of an overhaul.' Deliberately, he let his gaze rake over her crumpled dress, at the sting of colour which still flushed her face. 'Tell me, did you have sex with me because you thought it would put you in a *better* bargaining position—because if I were you, I would really rethink your strategy in future, *cara*. Your worth would be greatly enhanced if you withheld the sex until *after* you had agreed the price.'

That did it. Her rage so blinding, her fury and her frustration and sense of self-recrimination were all so overwhelming that Emma just flew across the suite, launching herself at him, raining a battery of blows at the unforgiving wall of his chest.

But Vincenzo merely laughed, capturing her drumming little fists easily within the restraining grasp of his hands and stilling her with a contemptuous curve of his lips as he brought his mouth up close to her ear.

'Did you imagine that such a spirited display would have me eating out of your hand?' he whispered. 'Or eating you?'

'Vincenzo!'

'Vincenzo!' he mocked. And *wasn't* the fiercely hot kick of desire hitting him hard in the groin—and didn't he just want to press it against her warm, soft mound, to seek a quick and urgent release from this infernal desire? But sex without strings was one thing—having sex with her after what she had just told him was something entirely different.

Dropping his hands from her as if she were contaminated, he walked over to the other side of the room, his back facing her. People always said that Vincenzo's face was cold and shuttered—that working out what was going on in his head from the look on his face was like trying to read a stone. But Emma was better at it than most because inevitably she knew him better than most. And so he needed to be careful.

Staring out of the window, he studied the dark gleam of the river and the dazzling light from the buildings which were reflected on its rippling surface. Logic told him that she was lying—and it also told him that if she persisted with her crazy contention, then he should simply refer it to his lawyers. It wasn't exactly unheard of for fabulously wealthy men to be hit on by women with spurious paternity claims—but these days, fortunately, there were the means to establish the truth in such a claim.

He should tell her to get out, to leave the suite now—and he should put someone onto it in the morning. Why, he need not even meet with her again—it could all be put into the hands of his legal experts.

But some instinct made Vincenzo loath to follow the voice of logic, and he wasn't sure why. Was it because the sex between them had been utter dynamite—just as it always had been with her—and because it had awoken in him a hunger which she could feed better than any other woman he'd ever known?

Wouldn't it make more sense to play along with her—so that he could enjoy her body for a little longer before they parted for good? And wouldn't renewed evidence of her duplicity finally help dull the magic enchantment which she could still wield over his senses?

Turning back, he surprised her chewing on her bottom lip like a nervous exam candidate. So was she? Nervous? Of course she was.

'Where do you live?' he questioned.

'In a little place called Boisdale—it's about an hour's drive from here.'

'Did you drive here today?'

Still smarting from all the hurt and the pain—some of it admittedly self-inflicted—Emma wondered which planet he lived on, until she remembered. He lived on Planet Wealth. Vincenzo had guessed that she was short of money, but someone in his position would have no idea of what that would mean in real terms. To him, being broke might mean having a pretty standard car—the idea that she would simply be unable to pay for road tax and petrol, let alone the cost of learning to drive would be completely outside his experience.

'No, I still haven't got my licence,' she said, just wanting to get away now and as soon as possible. Away from that disdainful face and the memory of what she had just allowed to happen. All she wanted was to wash away every trace of him… She would blow the expense, put the immersion heater on and submerge herself in a hot, deep bath the minute she got home. 'No, I came by train.'

Emma glanced at her watch, but the blur of numbers danced in front of her eyes. At least she had told him, and he hadn't believed her. Gino would be unable to blame her and maybe this was all for the best. She need never see him again and she would manage. Somehow. 'And, in fact, I ought to be getting back.'

'Yes. I will order a car,' said Vincenzo, sliding his mobile phone from his pocket.

'That won't be necessary, thank you. I'll be fine.'

'You think perhaps I am playing the gentleman,

cara?' he taunted silkily, with a shake of his dark head. 'Alas, you are mistaken. You may be content to take public transport, but I can assure you that I am not.'

Emma stared at him, putting her confusion and interpretation of mixed messages down to the fact that she was tired and aching. 'I don't quite understand what you mean.'

'Don't you?' questioned Vincenzo softly. 'Haven't you realised that I shall be coming with you?'

Emma stared at him in alarm. 'What, you mean—to Boisdale? But I thought…'

'What did you think?' he put in as her strained whisper faded into an open-mouthed look of disbelief.

'That you didn't believe me.'

'I don't.' His mouth hardened as he punched out a number on his phone, and said something swiftly in his Sicilian dialect, before meeting her gaze with cold, hard eyes. 'But the easiest way to rule out a whole load of unnecessary paperwork and time is to see the baby for myself.'

'You think you'll be able to establish his paternity just by looking at him?'

'Of course I do. The Cardini genes are unmistakable,' he said, his voice harsh as he called her bluff. 'You know that as well as I do.'

Emma swallowed. 'He'll be asleep.'

So now she had backed herself into a corner. 'So much the better—for I have no wish to unsettle the child.' A low beeping sound emitting from his phone alerted his attention and he shot Emma a disparaging glance. 'Now put your shoes back on, *cara*—and let's get this over with. The car's here.'

CHAPTER SEVEN

IT WAS the journey from hell.

Despite the quietly opulent luxury of Vincenzo's chauffeur-driven car, Emma sat bolt upright on the soft leather seat as if she were facing a firing squad. Yet that was exactly how it felt—only she happened to be facing the lethal weapons of his words rather than the cold metal of a gun.

But if she stopped to think about it—what had she really expected to happen? She knew what kind of man Vincenzo was—had she really imagined that he would just calmly accept such a momentous piece of information from her? Perhaps that he would just nod sagely and give her a divorce and then politely ask when it might be convenient for him to visit his son? As if.

What a fool she had been not to have anticipated this.

But at least this way it would soon be all over and there would be no awful delay to endure. No feeling threatened while she waited anxiously to see just what he would do next. Vincenzo would soon set eyes on

Gino and would know instantly that the baby had sprung from *his* loins. Emma knotted her fingers together. And of course *that* would bring up problems all of its own—but at least she would have done the right thing, and after the initial anger had subsided, surely they were mature enough to work out some kind of effective compromise.

'So who has been looking after him today?'

The question shot at her from out of the gloom and somehow her estranged husband had managed to turn it into an accusation. 'My friend Joanna.'

'I see.' In the dim light Vincenzo's mouth twisted, but Emma noticed, as no doubt he had intended her to do. 'She is experienced in the care of children?'

'She's got a little boy about the same age,' Emma put in hastily, hating the fact that she felt the need to defend herself and yet wanting to impress on him that she *was* a good mother. 'And she's brilliant with him. This evening she's left her son with her husband so that she could put mine to bed in his own home.'

A long finger drummed a slightly menacing little beat on the taut surface of one tensile thigh. 'So tell me, Emma—how often do you leave your child with someone else while you go off to London to have casual sex?'

It was a bitter and damning allegation and Emma felt her body begin to shake with the injustice of it. She shook her head and stared up into his face, unable to help the indignant tremble of her lips. 'How *dare* you say something like that?'

'You mean, that the way you behaved today with me isn't the way you usually behave with men?'

'You know damned well it isn't!'

Yes, deep down he knew that. It had been evident in the hungry way she had responded to him today—and in the general and conflicting air of untouchability which she had always possessed. Hadn't it been that very quality which had first so ensnared him and which had made him lose control more times than he cared to remember?

But Vincenzo was a Sicilian man—and that carried with it a whole lot of complex issues about how women should and shouldn't behave when it came to sex. Back there in the Vinoly suite, Emma had behaved with the wild abandon of a mistress—not a young mother who had left her baby for the day with someone who wasn't family! And although he had revelled in the experience they had just shared, there was a part of him which also despised it.

Vincenzo turned his head to stare at the darkened English countryside which was rushing past the window, watching as the car slowed and then passed through a surprisingly impressive entrance gate, before making its way up a wide, tree-lined drive. On the far horizon, he could see an imposing-looking house which stood in an elevated position, all lit up and glowing golden.

'You live *here*?' he demanded.

For one moment, Emma was so tempted to tell him that, yes, she did. That really she was simply *pretend-*

ing to be hard-up as some kind of diversion in order to amuse herself!

'Hardly,' she said drily. 'I rent a cottage in the grounds. It's over there. Can you tell the chauffeur to turn to the right and then travel straight on past the lake?'

Vincenzo clicked on the intercom and spoke to the driver in rapid Italian as the limousine changed direction. It purred its way to a smooth halt in front of March Cottage and he found his eyes narrowing in surprise, for this was not what he had been expecting, either.

It was tiny; one of those cute little houses which always seemed to feature on the front of postcards—with its stone walls and some sort of leafy thing scrambling around the front door, over which hung an old-fashioned lantern.

Although a gust of cold wind whirled round them as they stepped from the car, Emma's palms were clammy with sweat as she turned to him, wondering what was going on behind that forbidding profile as he stared up at the front of the cottage. 'I'd better go in first and warn—'

'No.' The word silenced her just as much as the hand placed lightly on her forearm, his fingers curling briefly around her tiny wrist. He saw her blue eyes darken, and widen. His voice dipped to a silky threat. 'You do not need to warn anyone, *cara mia*. Come, I will accompany you.'

Emma felt trapped—but presumably that was what he had intended—and yet why on earth *should* she feel trapped? This was *her* territory now, not his. He was only here because he wanted to convince himself that the baby was not his. *Well, you are in for the shock of a lifetime, Signor Cardini*, she thought fiercely.

'Hello!' she called, pushing open the door, and saw a light coming from the sitting room.

Joanna was lying on the sofa, wrapped up in a blanket and watching TV—a banana skin and an empty coffee cup on the floor beside her. 'It's bloody freezing,' she complained as Emma walked in and then her face froze into a look of utter disbelief when she registered the rugged olive face of the man who was following her.

Pushing the blanket off, she sat up immediately. 'Ooh! Good grief! You must be—'

'This is Vincenzo Cardini,' said Emma without any further explanation, giving Joanna an I'll-tell-you-everything-later look. 'How's he been?'

Joanna appeared to judge the look correctly, though Emma saw her shooting curious glances at the tall, dark man who stood dominating the small space with a moody look. 'Oh, no trouble really,' she said. 'Though he didn't really want to settle—missing his mum, I guess. But he ate an enormous tea and afterwards I gave him a bath—though you really ought to see about getting Andrew to install a heater in the bathroom, Emma.'

'Andrew?' questioned Vincenzo dangerously. 'And just who is Andrew?'

'Andrew is my landlord,' said Emma quickly.

Black eyes bored into her. 'Oh, is he?'

She wanted to say that Andrew's identity was none

of his business, but she had *made* it his business, in a way—first by allowing herself to be intimate with him, and then by announcing that he was the father of her child. Given Vincenzo's track record with jealousy and possession, was it any wonder that he looked like a volcano just about to erupt?

Joanna jumped up. 'Look, I'd better get off home.'

Emma nodded and flashed her friend a grateful smile. 'Thanks, Jo—I really appreciate it and I'll see you tomorrow.'

There was an uncomfortable kind of silence while Joanna picked up her coat and bag and went to reach for the discarded banana skin.

'Oh, don't worry about that,' said Emma quickly.

'I'll let myself out, then,' said Joanna.

But Emma barely heard her go. She felt rooted to the spot—not knowing what the hell she should do next—but it seemed that Vincenzo had no such problems with indecision.

'Where is he?' he demanded.

'In…in there.' She pointed at the bedroom door, which was slightly ajar, noticing almost dispassionately that her finger was shaking. 'Please don't wake him.'

Vincenzo's mouth twisted into a mocking parody of a smile. 'I have no desire to wake him. Believe me when I tell you that this is simply to put my mind at rest. One look and I'm out of here. Just show me the child.'

It was the most bizarre of all situations, creeping into Gino's bedroom, her heart frozen with fear and love, trying to see him as Vincenzo would be seeing him—as if for the first time in the soft glow of the night-light. And, no matter what lay ahead, Emma felt the sharp rush of maternal pride as she gazed down on her son.

He was lying on his back, little fisted arms bunched up alongside his head—as if he were spoiling for a fight. As usual, he had managed to kick off his covers and automatically Emma moved forward to pull it back over him.

'No.' Vincenzo's word stopped her. 'Leave it.'

'But—'

'I said, *leave it.*'

Her breath caught in her throat, Emma watched as Vincenzo walked slowly to the side of the cot, ducking his dark head and only narrowly avoiding missing the animal mobile which was swirling madly around above it.

For a moment Vincenzo just stood there, staring down—as motionless and as formidable as a statue constructed from some cold, dark ebony.

Emma felt her fingernails digging into her palms, wanting to break the spell of this terrible and uneasy situation, but somehow not daring to. This was his right, she realised—to take as long as he liked.

With a fast-beating heart, Vincenzo committed the scene to memory. The riot of dark curls and the rather petulant curl of the sleeping mouth, which was so like the one which stared back at him from the mirror each morning when he was shaving. Though the light was dim, nothing could disguise the unmistakably golden-olive glow of the child's perfect skin—nor the hint of height and strength lying dormant in his baby frame.

Vincenzo expelled a long breath of air—the harsh sound penetrating the stillness in the room like an over-pumped tyre which had just been punctured. And then, without any kind of warning, he turned and walked from the room.

Emma fussed around, straightening the covers and feathering her fingertips through the silken mop of Gino's hair—almost as if she were willing him to wake up. But he was deeply asleep—worn out, no doubt— and she could not continue to hide here like some kind of fugitive, just to escape Vincenzo's wrath.

And you haven't done anything wrong, she told herself.

She walked back into the sitting room, where Vincenzo was standing waiting for her with the grim body language of an executioner, his black eyes filled with a cold look of rage.

His mouth twisted as the word was wrenched from him like bitter and deadly poison. *'Puttanesca!'*

As an insult it happened to be grossly inaccurate— but Emma knew that it was the macho insult of choice whenever a woman was considered to have wronged.

'I am not a whore,' she answered quietly. 'You know that. That's a cheap slur to make.'

His voice was equally quiet. 'Maybe I knew it was the only one you would understand.'

Their eyes met in the most honest moment of com-munication they'd had all day and Emma could have wept at the way he was trying to hurt her. This whole scenario had been intended as a *solution*—and yet it seemed to have spawned a rash of unsightly problems of its own along the way, and she couldn't for the life of her work out how they were going to come to some sort of compromise.

Vincenzo had dragged his gaze from her white face and was looking around him now, as if barely able to believe the surroundings in which he found himself. The faded sofa with a faint white frill where some of the stuffing was spilling out. The tired paintwork and the pale rectangles on the wall where pictures must once have hung and then been removed. The overriding sense that this was simply somewhere temporary—a place for life's losers.

'You…dare to bring my son up in a place like this?' he questioned unsteadily. 'To condemn him to a life of poverty.'

So he had not disputed the paternity claim! Relief washed over her but was quickly replaced with fear. And curiosity.

'So you accept that he's yours?'

Vincenzo chose his words carefully. He had expected to walk into the nursery and to see a baby—and to feel nothing more than he would feel for any baby. And perhaps there would have been a flare of jealousy, too—at being forced to confront the physical evidence that the woman he had married had been intimate with another man.

But it had not been like that. In fact, it had been like nothing he could ever have imagined. Because he had known immediately. On some subliminal level it had been instant—as if he had been programmed to recognise this little boy. He had seen photos of himself as a baby—and the similarity between himself and this infant was undeniable. But it was more than that. Something unknown had whipped at his heart as he'd looked down at that sleeping infant. Some primeval recognition. Some bond stretching back through the ages, as well as a blood line to take him into the unknown future.

'What is his name?' he demanded as he realised he *didn't even know* his son's name.

'Gino.'

'Gino,' he repeated softly. 'Gino.'

He said it quite differently from the way she did—pronounced it as it was probably intended to be pronounced—but the expression on his face belied the slight sense of wonder in his tone. There was something so forbiddingly unfamiliar about the way he was looking at her—something so icy cold and critical as his gaze swept over her. And Emma knew that she had to be strong—hadn't she told herself that first thing this morning, at the beginning of a day which seemed to have stretched on for an eternity? She must not let him intimidate her.

'So where do we go from here?' she asked.

His eyes narrowed. She was still wearing her coat. So was he—but only a fool would remove it in these sub-zero temperatures. Was his son warm enough? Gino. This time he tried the word out in his mind and a dark swirl of unknown emotion began to weave distorting patterns around his heart.

Suddenly he stepped forward, his hand snaking out to bring her up close and hard into the heat of his body, her fragility sending his senses into overdrive. His free hand roved over her bottom, feeling its faint curve beneath the soft wool, splaying his fingers there as his heart began to pound, his arousal soaring as he ground its hard heat against her. 'Feel how much I want you?' he grated.

'Vincenzo!'

There was a bleak and glittering look of finality in the black eyes before he drove his mouth down on hers and this time his kiss was punishing; angry. If kisses were supposed to be demonstrations of love, then this was their very antithesis. But that didn't stop her responding to it—Emma couldn't seem to prevent herself, no matter how much the voice of reason screamed in her ears to try.

And wasn't there some primeval sense that the man who held her was the acknowledged father of her child? Now that he had seen Gino, seen him and accepted him—hadn't that somehow forged some kind of unbreakable bond between the three of them? Some ancient, golden trinity which had been completed by Gino's birth. *Oh, you fool, Emma*, she told herself. *Inventing fantasies because they'll make you feel better about doing...this...*

'Vincenzo!' she moaned, opening her mouth beneath his—feeling his masculine heat and sensing the urgent tang of his desire. He had started to unbutton her coat now, and she was letting him. Just letting him push the fabric aside and skim his palms down over her hips. And now he was rucking her dress up, brushing his way negligently up to the apex of her thighs, and Emma felt herself wriggle impatiently, scraping her own hands across the broad reach of his shoulders, wanting to rip the coat away from him. Wishing that all their clothes could disappear, as if by magic. 'Vincenzo,' she said, again—more urgently this time.

He felt the plunder of his mouth on hers, the fierce thunder of his heart—his body so hard that he felt he might die if he didn't plunge deep inside her molten softness. For a second he responded to her. Circled his hips against hers in a provocative and primitive enticement as old as time, and she swayed against him, as if he were sucking her towards him with some magnetic and irresistible force. He could rip her panties off as she liked them to be ripped, could straddle her until she screamed and bucked beneath him.

And then, as abruptly as he had caught her close to him, Vincenzo dropped his hands and let her go—not reacting when he saw her knees buckle, her hand reach out to grasp the arm of the sofa, to steady herself.

'What am I thinking of?' he questioned, as if speaking to himself, his voice distorted by the sound of self-disgust. Hadn't he been tempted just then to do it to her one more time—despite the fact that she had kept his son hidden from him? To maybe dismiss the driver and take her to bed for the night and wake up in the morning to the sound of his son?

But wouldn't that weaken his bargaining position if she sapped his appetite with her sweet sexuality tonight? And if he left her now, he would leave her aching, and wondering… For Vincenzo knew that surprise was the most effective element of all when you were bargaining hard for something.

'Ah, Emma,' he said in a voice of molten steel. 'Too many times I have listened to my body where you are concerned, *mia bella*. Too many times have you used your pale sorcery to ensnare my body and to make me so hungry with need that I cannot think straight, but not now. For this is too important. Now I need to think with my head, instead of with my…'

His mouth twisted as a quick, downward glance indicated the source of his discomfort and he saw the flush of colour which flared along her cheekbones. How could she still blush like an innocent virgin, even while she had just been writhing in his arms like a red-hot alley cat? He stepped back from her, further away from her temptation, his face growing shuttered. 'I shall return here tomorrow morning, at nine.'

Something in his voice alerted her to trouble. Real trouble. 'Return for *what*, exactly?' questioned Emma, trying to keep her own voice calm.

He raked his hand back through his tousled black

hair. Wouldn't she just love to know what was going on in his mind? 'You'll just have to wait and see,' he declared softly.

CHAPTER EIGHT

EMMA spent a long, sleepless night—wondering how she could have been so stupid as to let herself be seduced by Vincenzo and lay herself open to all kinds of misinterpretation. She *knew* what his whole crazy, Sicilian attitude towards women was like. He would have considered her to have behaved wantonly—hadn't that much been obvious in the icy way he had looked at her? From the way he had dropped his hands from her body as if he had been holding something dirty and contaminated?

He clearly felt nothing but contempt for her, and if she continued to behave in a way which would only increase that view, then she was just weakening her own position.

Because she should never for a moment forget who she was up against; a man who represented the full might of one of the richest and most powerful families in Sicily. She had seen the light of battle flare in his black eyes—and Emma wasn't stupid. She had something which Vincenzo had yearned for all his adult life—his son and heir—and if they were no longer together as man and wife, then wouldn't he go all out to try to win custody?

As the pale light of dawn crept through the curtains she pulled the duvet close round her shivering body wondering how she could ever have been so naïve not to have anticipated this. Had she thought when she first went to him that Vincenzo might behave like a civilised human being—when he had never behaved with a shred of civility in his life? Because everything was black and white in Vincenzo's world. Women were sluts or they were virgins. Mistresses or wives. And she was never going to be able to change that.

So what would he do next?

As she climbed wearily from her bed, she tried to put herself in the mindset of her estranged husband. Would he try to prove her as an unfit mother? Would he attempt to use against her the very thing that she had gone to him for help with?

Pulling on a pair of old jeans and the thickest sweater she could find, Emma washed her face and hands and then went into the kitchen to make herself a cup of coffee before Gino awoke.

He slept later than usual. Which was absolutely typical, she thought. The one time she could have had a bit of a lie-in and here she was—prowling around the cottage, her nerves stretched tight as an elastic band, unable to settle to anything until at last Gino woke and she was able to hug his warm little body close to her.

She was mashing up some banana for his breakfast when the doorbell rang and she suddenly realised that she hadn't even brushed her hair properly. Still, at least Vincenzo wouldn't think that she was going on an all-out effort to...to... Emma frowned. How had he put it? To use her *pale sorcery*. But that was the trouble with Vincenzo—even when he was insulting you, he put it in such a way that it made you want to melt when you thought about it afterwards.

So don't *think about it*, she told herself fiercely as she pulled open the door, her defensive expression dying when she saw it was Andrew standing there, a bowl of eggs in his hand and a rather rueful expression on his face.

'Morning, Emma,' he said gruffly, holding the bowl out. 'I've brought you these. One of the farmers sent them over and I thought you might like them.'

Emma blinked. 'Oh. Well, thanks, Andrew—how lovely. We'll have them for tea.'

He was looking rather pink about the ears. 'Er, is it all right if I come in for a minute?'

Surreptitiously, Emma glanced at her watch. It was still before nine—Vincenzo was unlikely to turn up this early. And even if he did, she was separated from him, wasn't she? She happened to have a *life*—and that life didn't include him or his old-fashioned view on how she should live it.

'Of course,' she said brightly. 'I'm just about to feed Gino—do you want to put the kettle on and we can have a cuppa?'

He filled the kettle up and then turned to her, shifting from one foot to the other as if he were standing on something hot. 'It's just that I feel bad about announcing a rent increase when I know you can't really afford it. So why don't we forget we ever had that conversation?'

Emma blinked. 'Forget it?'

'Sure. After all,' he continued, with a shrug, 'you're a good tenant—and the place is pretty ropey, really. You can carry on as you were, Emma—I shan't mind.'

Emma turned her grimace into a smile as she poured out two steaming mugs full of tea and handed him one and then sat down to start feeding Gino. If only he had told her this before—then she needn't have ever gone to Vincenzo, cap in hand and asking for some kind of divorce settlement.

But that wasn't really true, was it? She had needed to speak to Vincenzo some time and maybe the rent increase had just brought matters to a head. She couldn't keep running away from him all her life, burying her head in the sand and avoiding the inevitable—because it had been inevitable that Gino would one day meet his father.

But at least Andrew's words had taken the sting and the urgency out of her situation. Removed that terrible, tearing feeling of panic.

'That's very sweet of you, Andrew—and I appreciate it.'

'No. Don't mention it,' he said gruffly, stirring his tea for a moment before looking up, his eyes curious. 'One of the groundsmen said there was a big car here last night.'

Emma's paused, the banana midway to Gino's mouth, before he grabbed for the spoon himself. 'Is there something written into my tenancy agreement which forbids that?' she questioned lightly as she helped him spoon it in.

'Of course not. It's just that you don't often have visitors, and I—' His head jerked up.

Gino's squawk from the high chair meant that Emma hadn't heard the knock at the door until it was repeated loudly—and so she barely noticed that Gino was shoving a fistful of pureed banana into her hair.

'There's someone at the door,' said Andrew unnecessarily.

She wanted to tell him to leave—to spirit him away, or smuggle him out of the back door, until she realised that she was thinking like a madwoman. Hadn't she vowed to be strong? *So stop acting as if you're doing something wrong.* Andrew was her landlord and he had a perfect right to be here.

She pulled the door open to find Vincenzo standing there and her heart leapt in her chest. For this was a casual Vincenzo—a different creature entirely from the office billionaire who had seduced her so effectively yesterday. Today he was dressed in dark jeans and a dark jacket. An outwardly relaxed Vincenzo—and somehow all the more dangerous for that. Like a snake asleep in the sun who, when disturbed, would lift its head and stare at you with its deadly and unblinking eyes.

'Good morning,' she said, thinking that the very greeting was a complete fabrication—because what was good about this particular morning?

He didn't acknowledge the welcome—his gaze instead flicking over her shoulder to survey the scene behind her. The baby sitting in a high chair, surrounded by mess—his attention caught by the noise at the door—and he was staring directly at Vincenzo, his dark brown eyes huge in his face.

Vincenzo felt a hot, almost painful curve around his heart as he stared back at the little boy with the same fascinated interest. But he was inhibited from doing what he really wanted, which was to walk straight over there and to pluck him out of the high chair, because there was a man—yes, a *man*—sitting in Emma's kitchen with his feet underneath her table and drinking a cup of tea. What was more, he had not risen to his feet as one of Vincenzo's employees would have done.

'And who the hell are you?' he demanded icily.

'I *beg* your pardon?' said Andrew.

'You heard me. Who are you and what are you doing here, in my wife's kitchen?'

'Your *wife*?' Andrew jumped to his feet and turned to Emma—his expression one of dismay and accusation. 'But you told me your husband wasn't on the scene any more!'

'Oh, did she?' came the dark, silky question from the other side of the room.

This was like a bad dream, thought Emma. She swallowed. 'I think perhaps it's best if you go now, Andrew.'

Andrew frowned. 'You're sure you'll be okay?'

It was sweet of him to have asked—but, with a slight feeling of hysteria, Emma wondered what solution her landlord was about to offer to help get her out of this situation. Throw the simmering Sicilian off the premises perhaps—when he looked like some dark and immovable force? She managed a smile. 'I'll be fine,' she said reassuringly.

An awkward kind of silence descended while Andrew let himself out of the front door and the moment it had closed behind him Vincenzo turned to her, his face a study in repressed fury.

'You have been sleeping with him?' he demanded in a low voice, aware that there was a child in the room.

Angrily, she flushed. 'What do you think?'

'I think that he does not look man enough to cope with your voracious sexual appetite, *cara*—although it might explain why you were so unbelievably hot for me.' His black eyes scorched into her. 'But you haven't answered my question.'

'Of course I haven't been sleeping with him,' she breathed, hurt and indignant and shaking. But he had now turned away—as if he couldn't care less what the answer was. As if asking it had been nothing but careless sport designed to embarrass and humiliate her. And he had managed, hadn't he? Achieved just that with flying colours.

Instead, he was walking towards the high chair, where Gino was still staring up at him with the engrossed attention which an eager member of the audience might give to a stage hypnotist.

He stood looking down at him for one long, immeasurable moment while his heart struck out a hard and heavy beat. *'Mio figlio,'* he said eventually in a voice which was distorted with pain and joy. 'My son.'

Inwardly, Emma flinched at the raw possession in his voice even as she marvelled that Gino—*her* son—was not backing away from Vincenzo, the way he usually did with strangers.

But Vincenzo is not a stranger, is he? He is as close a blood relative as you are. And maybe Gino recognises that on some subliminal level.

'Vene,' Vincenzo was saying softly, holding out his hands. 'Come.'

To Emma's astonishment, the baby blinked and played coy a couple of times—leaning back against the plastic chair and turning his head from this way to that as he fixed Vincenzo with a sideways glance. But Vincenzo didn't push him, just continued to murmur to him in the soft, distinctive Sicilian accent until at last Gino wriggled a little and allowed Vincenzo to scoop him out of the high chair and into his arms.

Gino was letting someone he'd only just met pick him up and cuddle him! Emma's world swayed. She felt sick, faint and, yes…*jealous*. That Vincenzo should so effortlessly win the affection of everyone he wanted.

'He…he needs a wash,' she said shakily, blinking her eyes furiously against the sudden prick of tears, barely able to believe what she was witnessing.

There was a pause as Vincenzo flicked his gaze over her. At her matted hair and pale face—broken only by two spots of colour at the centre of her cheeks. At the faded jeans and bare feet—worn with a bulky sweater, which so cleverly concealed the petite curves which lay beneath.

He did not know of another woman who would dare to appear before him in such a careless state, and when he looked at her objectively, it was hard to believe that she was his wife. And yet those big blue eyes still had the power to kick savagely at his groin. To twist him up inside. 'And so do you, by the look of it,' he bit out.

Knowing that she was about to cry, Emma fled into the bathroom—locking the door behind her—and turning on the shower to drown the muffled sound of her shuddered breathing. She let the water cascade down onto her face to mingle with her tears as her troubled thoughts spun round like a washing machine. What had she done? What had she *done*? Opened the floodgates to Vincenzo's involvement—not just in her life, but in the life of Gino, too. And he had come rushing in with a great dark swamp of power and possession.

At least there was enough water in the antiquated tank for it to be piping hot—and as she washed the banana out of her hair it struck her that for once she was not running against the clock. She normally showered while Gino was sleeping, and often the water was tepid.

Of course, in her distress she hadn't brought a change of clothes in with her. So she wrapped herself in the biggest bath towel and wound a smaller one around her damp hair and self-consciously walked back through to reach her bedroom, steeling herself to see Vincenzo in her sitting room. But he hadn't even noticed her come in. He had other, far more important things on his mind.

Still carrying Gino, he was walking around the small room, stopping to peer at small objects—a photo of her mother here, a little clock she'd inherited there. And all the while he was speaking softly to Gino in Sicilian, and, directly afterwards, in English. And Gino was listening, fascinated—occasionally lifting his chubby little finger to touch the dark, rasping shadow of his father's jaw.

He's teaching him Sicilian, Emma realised, acknowledging the sudden bolt of fear which shot through her. But standing wrapped in a towel was no way to remonstrate with him, even if remonstration was an option—which she guessed it wasn't, not really.

Black eyes looked up over the silky tangle of Gino's head and met hers and he found anger vying with desire. But there was a child in his arms, a child who would be confused and frightened by any display of anger, and so Vincenzo forced himself to ask her a cool question. 'Good shower?'

'Lovely, thank you.'

He held her gaze as he let desire in. 'I can imagine,' he said softly, eyes now drifting to the soft swell of her breasts visibly curving beneath the thin material of cheap towel.

Now she was shivering with more than cold and Emma turned her back on him, hating the mixed messages he was sending out to her and the way they were making her feel. It was as if he wanted to weaken her in every way he could—first, by being proprietorial with Gino and then by that unspoken, sensual scrutiny. She felt in a complete muddle—as if the Emma of yesterday had disappeared and now a stranger had taken her place.

She dressed quickly, choosing a pair of clean jeans and a different sweater; her normal, daily, practical and presentable uniform, which never in a million years could be described as flattering. But Emma was glad. She was unwilling to 'dress up'—to look as if she might be trying to make an impression on him. Or have him accuse her of playing the temptress again.

Only when she'd brushed her hair and given it a quick blast of the dryer did she take in a deep breath and go back into the sitting room, where Vincenzo was now standing with his back to her, holding Gino and looking out down the garden at the spreading chestnut tree, as she herself had done a million times before.

Gino heard her first, for he turned in his father's arms and then gave a little squawk and began to wriggle towards her and Emma held out her arms and took her son, burying her face in his curls to hide the great rush of unknown emotion which was threatening to swamp her.

His arms empty without the baby's warm weight, Vincenzo walked back towards the window, his heart beating very loud and very strong, more shaken than he had anticipated. And when he turned to look at Emma, to look at her cradling the child in what he considered to be a completely over-the-top way, his mouth hardened.

She glanced up, trying to read his expression but failing as she encountered a stony black gaze which gave absolutely nothing away. But why should that surprise her? Apart from those first few, heady months—when they had been rocked by the power of sexual attraction masquerading as love—she never *had* been able to tell what was going on in that head of his. He didn't ever tell her. He didn't *do* confidences, he'd once told her. As if talking about feelings made a man look weak.

'Do you have any coffee?' he questioned unexpectedly.

She felt wrong-footed. 'Probably not the kind you're used to. I keep it in the fridge,' she said, and then pointed at one of the kitchen cupboards. 'There's a cafetiere in there.'

'So you have not adopted the foul, instant-coffee habit of your countrymen,' observed Vincenzo caustically as he began to set about making a pot with the air of a man to whom the kitchen was unfamiliar territory.

Emma watched him, wondering how he did it. She knew that he had always had women waiting on him hand and foot all his life. Quite frankly, she was surprised he hadn't demanded that *she* make his coffee for him, except that even Vincenzo probably didn't dare try *that*. But how quickly he adapted, she thought reluctantly. To see him now, you would imagine that he had been making morning coffee since he was first permitted to put a flame beneath a pot.

So why couldn't he have adapted to married life so easily instead of embracing such an old-fashioned and autocratic relationship? It was as if by slipping that gold band onto her finger he had stepped back by a few decades.

Emma put Gino down onto the patchwork mat she'd finished off in those last, tiring days of her pregnancy and put down his large cardboard box for him to play with. She had covered it with wrapping paper and filled it with washed and empty plastic containers of different sizes—some of them filled with beans and rice, which made varying sounds.

Vincenzo paused in the act of pouring out two cups of coffee, his lips curving in derision. 'Why is he playing with rubbish?' he demanded.

'It's a home-made toy,' defended Emma, standing her ground. 'He watched me make it—so it was educational. He even turns it into a drum kit by banging a wooden spoon against it! And children often appreciate a simple plaything more than an expensive one.'

'Which presumably you can't afford anyway?' he challenged.

Emma shrugged. 'Well, no.'

Vincenzo glanced around him, not bothering to hide his distaste as he sank onto one of the hard chairs around the dining table. 'Can't afford very much at all by the look of things,' he observed, and then put his cup down and his eyes lanced through her with a look of pure black ice. 'Which presumably is what brought you back to me.'

She didn't feel that now was the right time to correct him. To tell him that nothing had brought her *back to him*. That this was about the legal ending of their ill-fated marriage, and nothing to do with feelings. 'I wanted the best for Gino,' she said in a low voice.

'Did you really, Emma?' he queried silkily. 'Or did you just think you'd try to screw me for as much money as possible?' His eyes glittered. 'As well as screw me in other ways.'

Colour flared in her cheeks. 'Don't be so coarse!' she whispered, as if Gino might be able to understand his crude allusion and judge his mother to be morally corrupt. *And aren't you?* prompted the voice of her conscience. *Was it really appropriate behaviour to do what you did with your estranged husband in the Vinoly suite yesterday?*

Vincenzo shrugged and carried on as if she hadn't spoken. His tone was soft—presumably not to alarm Gino—but that did nothing to detract from the venom which underpinned it. 'If you'd really wanted the best for him, then you would have contacted me a long time ago.'

'But I tried,' she protested. 'I tried to ring you and you refused to take my call! Twice!'

'Then you didn't try hard enough, did you?' he snapped. 'Just enough to go through the motions, but with no real determination. But that probably suited you very well, didn't it, Emma, since everything seems to have been satisfying *your* needs, *cara*—and your desires?'

She stared at him, shocked by the bitterness in his voice.

'And it's *still* about your desires, isn't it?' he continued remorselessly. 'You came to me because you wanted money and wanted sex—and so far you've scored on one count.'

'I did *not* come to you for sex!'

'No?' he queried witheringly. 'Someone forced you to end up naked on the sofa with me, did they?' His eyes blazed. 'But nowhere in your schemes do you seem to have considered what the *child's* needs might be—'

'But I *did*!' Emma flared.

'Liar.' He leaned forward. 'You didn't think that it might have been a good idea to tell me about it when you discovered you were pregnant?'

'It isn't—'

'Or maybe when you went into labour, that I might like to have known?' His words ruthlessly cut through her stumbled explanation. 'Or when you'd given birth—that as the father I had an inalienable and unquestionable *right* to know about it. Didn't that occur to you, Emma?'

'We've been through all this,' she said dully. 'Even if you *had* shown me the courtesy of taking my calls, you wouldn't have believed me.'

'Not at first, perhaps,' he agreed through gritted teeth. 'But just as I'm doing now, I would eventually have come around to realising that we *had* conceived a child—even if it did happen to be in the most unfortunate circumstances possible.'

Emma flinched, feeling for Gino. 'Please don't talk about it in that way.'

'But it is true, *cara*.' His eyes mocked her. 'For surely even you would not deny that the circumstances surrounding his conception were regrettable?'

Regrettable. What a cruel yet emotionless word to use. What if she told him that her heart had been in bits that last day in Rome? That she had been aching and empty and longing for that sweet time to return, when all they had wanted or needed was love. That when he had pulled her into his arms as she'd been about to walk out of his life for good, she had been blown away by a passion which had seemed to mimic that time.

No, if she told him any of that, he would simply accuse her of lying again. Because, from the shuttered look of anger on his autocratic face, Emma could see that he had already made his mind up about her.

She couldn't help shivering as she put her coffee cup down on the table and stared at him, wondering what he was intending to do with his newly acquired knowledge.

'So…so what is going to happen now?' she questioned faintly. 'I'm assuming that you're going to want regular…access?'

He gave a short, disbelieving laugh. 'What do you think?'

She bit her lip. 'I don't know,' she whispered, but, knowing Vincenzo as she did, he was going to want to take it right to the limit. Would he want holidays in Sicily for Gino? she wondered painfully. An entrée into that harsh and beautiful world which would gradually exclude his pale English mother? She was going to have to be mature about this. To deal with it in a calm and re-flective way and then maybe Vincenzo would respond in the same way.

'How best...how best do you think we should we go about it?' she asked as politely as if she were asking a stranger the time of day.

Vincenzo had spent the last twelve hours thinking of nothing else. There was only one solution and it was one that he had felt with a powerful and bone-deep certainty.

'You will return with me to Sicily,' he said flatly, his voice as dark as his face.

'You must be out of your mind,' she breathed, 'if you really think I'd go anywhere near Sicily again.'

Vincenzo's lips curved into a cruel smile. Oh, but she was playing right into his hands! 'Then do not come,' he said softly. 'But in that case I shall take Gino myself.'

'T-take Gino?' Emma's heart was beating so fast and so loudly that she could barely hear her own reply. 'You seriously think I'd let you take my son out of the country without me?'

'*Our* son. Who has a history which will not be denied him. I intend on taking him to Sicily, Emma—and trying to stop me will seriously backfire against you in the long run.' He rose to his feet, moving as silently as a jungle cat to stand directly in front of her. 'I already have a team of lawyers working on the case, and let me tell you that they were singularly unimpressed by your efforts to conceal my son from me.'

He steeled his heart against the sudden blanching of her cheeks. Damn her—and her penchant for acting vulnerable whenever she thought it might help her case. His eyes gleamed. 'The more reasonable your behaviour now, then the more sympathetic I am likely to be towards you in the future.'

Emma swallowed. 'Are you...*threatening* me, Vincenzo?'

'Not at all. I'm simply advising you to be amenable—'

'You *are* threatening me—I knew you would! You haven't changed a bit! No wonder I—'

But her words were halted by the soft dig of Vincenzo's fingers into her arms as he hauled her to her feet, and his face swam in and out of her line of vision. 'The past is just that. Past,' he said flatly. 'It is the present which concerns me now and my son *is* the present, as well as the future. I am taking him with me and if you intend to accompany us, then you will play the part of my wife.'

She stared up at him. It was as if she had slipped and were falling deeper and deeper into a dark hole of Vincenzo's making. 'Your *wife*?'

Ebony eyes burned into her. 'Why not? It makes perfect sense.' He saw the look of confusion darkening her blue eyes and felt the flicker of a pulse at his temple. 'Let's just say that it will ease the tension of an already difficult situation,' he continued. 'We might as well enjoy what pleasures we can while we have the opportunity to do so.'

Emma felt weak. He sounded so cold-blooded—as if pleasure were nothing more than the by-product of a bodily function. 'You can't mean that.'

'Oh, but I can,' he promised, with grim satisfaction. 'And I think you could usefully lose the outraged attitude, don't you? In view of your response to me, you're in danger of looking a little like a hypocrite.'

'Vincenzo—'

'No. No more arguments, not any more. You've played according to your rules for long enough, Emma, and now it is time to play to some of mine.' His voice hardened. 'So pack the essentials and do it now, for we are going to London.'

Emma could tell from the obdurate look on his face and the flat tone of his voice that resistance would be futile. How could she possibly resist the powerhouse which was Vincenzo Cardini? But she had to try. 'Can't Gino and I wait here until we're ready to go?'

'And have you trying to run away from me?' His mouth curved into a sardonic representation of a smile as he ran a questing fingertip lightly over the sudden tremble of her lips. 'I think not. Do you have a passport?'

Dumbly, she nodded.

'Does Gino?'

'No.'

'Then I shall need to arrange that. And, besides, you

both need a new wardrobe. If I am taking you back to Sicily, then my son will look like a Cardini and not some little pauper. While you…' his eyes glittered with a look which simultaneously appalled and yet thrilled her '…you will dress to please me. As a wife should dress.'

CHAPTER NINE

EMMA stared round the vast salon of the Vinoly suite in disbelief.

There were clothes everywhere.

Clothes which looked exactly her size and precisely the colours that suited her. Beautiful clothes. Dresses and skirts. Spindly-heeled shoes. Bras and panties. All in the finest and most costly materials—silks and linens and pure, soft cashmere.

'Where on earth did these come from?' she asked in a low voice, wondering where he proposed she wear those outrageous shoes in a country like Sicily.

Vincenzo's black eyes hardened. 'I chose them—or, rather, I briefed someone with my specifications of what you would require for your trip to Sicily. I told you, Emma—you cannot and will not appear before my family dressed as a tramp.'

'But I've lost weight,' she whispered. 'A lot of weight. How on earth could you know what size I'd be?'

His slow smile belied his slightly incredulous expression that she should have asked such a guileless question. 'I guessed—or, rather, I assessed. Don't forget you were naked in my arms not so long ago.' Carelessly, he plucked a blue silk dress from the hanger and held it towards her. 'Here. Go and put this one on. I think you should dress for dinner, don't you?'

Emma found her fingers curling around the soft material, fighting the temptation to dress up, as he wanted her to. Part of her loved the clothes—what woman wouldn't, when she had worn cheap and second-hand stuff for so long? But his manner was alienating her and she had to accept that maybe his attitude was intentional. Determined that she should accept his generosity while drumming into her that she should never forget it was charity—and that everything in life always came at a price.

But did she really have a sensible alternative when Vincenzo's words had the harsh ring of truth about them? If she turned up in Sicily looking like a tramp as Vincenzo himself had so sweetly put it, she would win the sympathy of no one in a country where appearance was everything. Could she really face his family's critical gaze if she stubbornly insisted on wearing the few clothes she had flung into a suitcase before their hurried exit from the cottage earlier?

Especially as Gino had already been kitted out as befitted the son of a billionaire.

On the drive back from the cottage they had stopped off at one of London's biggest department stores and

Vincenzo had gone through it like a minesweeper. The finest clothes? Bought. The toughest yet most luxurious buggy? It was theirs. Cashmere blankets for the baby? Done.

She stared through into the bedroom at the beautiful cot which had been awaiting them on their return and where her beloved little boy now slept as soundly as a pampered prince and her heart turned over with guilt.

The Vinoly staff had been summoned to provide tea for the baby and afterwards he had squealed with delight as Vincenzo produced toy after expensive toy from a box, the like of which Gino had never seen. And although back at the cottage she had protested that babies were just as happy with a wooden spoon banging on the side of an old saucepan, now she could see that this was not quite true.

Even bath-time had been upmarket—his battered yellow duck forgotten in the face of the sleek little boat which bobbed over the fragrant surface of the water. Afterwards, Gino had been so exhausted that he had fallen asleep in Vincenzo's arms and a lump had risen in Emma's throat as she had watched him tenderly lay the child down in his cot.

On the one hand it was wonderful to see her baby enjoying the kind of comfort which every mother wanted for her child. To stare at Gino dressed in a cute and cosy sleep suit instead of layered up in the cheap vests and thin towelling which were his normal garb.

But even as she revelled in his obvious comfort, disturbing thoughts kept hitting her like a hammer-blow, wondering how she could possibly have denied him what was rightfully his for so long.

Her fingertips tightened around the soft blue silk dress. Wouldn't a refusal to wear it leave her looking like the hired help? 'Okay. I'll go and get changed,' she said.

'And dump those jeans while you're at it,' he suggested caustically. 'I don't ever want to see them again.'

His words stinging in her ears, Emma went into the bathroom and began to slither into her new clothes, feeling slightly awkward as the delicate lingerie came into contact with her skin and all her newly awoken senses.

She stared at herself in the mirror and it was like looking at a stranger. How long had it been since she'd treated herself to brand-new underwear and worn a decent bra which actually supported her? Or had matching lace-trimmed panties which made her feel both shy and yet decadent all at the same time?

The jeans which Vincenzo so despised lay in a crumpled heap on the bathroom floor and a last lingering flare of rebellion made Emma want to snatch them up and put them back on, along with her tatty old sweater. Behind their comforting bulk she felt safe from Vincenzo's sensual scrutiny—and you could hide behind such nondescript garments. But what was the point of adding fuel to the formidable fire of a man already angry enough?

Instead, she pulled the sleeved dress over her head and afterwards brushed her long hair so that it fell down in two shining blonde wings over her shoulders. The silk felt butter soft and hung in rich folds over her thighs and the colour brought out the blue of her eyes. This was how the wife of a rich man should dress, she realised. The way she always *used* to dress in those final empty days of their marriage—when she would be shown off like some pretty accessory in public, while at home the tensions between them grew and grew.

At least this time she was under no illusions that Vincenzo loved her—and surely that should enable her to adopt some kind of strategy for how to deal with him, and, more importantly, how to keep her emotions in check. Because there would be nothing but danger and trouble ahead for her and Gino if she allowed herself to fall under Vincenzo's charismatic spell once more.

She would play the part required of her while they negotiated some kind of settlement. But they would be doing it on *his* territory and a place where she had always felt like an outsider. Where she had *been* an outsider. She needed him on her side, she recognised with a sinking heart—but she needed to keep her *emotional* distance from him. At least these fancy clothes might act as a kind of armour—allowing her to fit into his wealthy world, externally if nothing else.

Stepping from the bathroom, she saw that Vincenzo had gone into the bedroom to look at Gino and he was standing beside the cot, and, despite everything, Emma found her heart turning over with longing. Sometimes the past could play terrible tricks with your mind and your heart. Sometimes you could feel as if you were still in love with the man you'd married.

Had he slept with many women since they'd split up? she found herself wondering painfully. Plunged deep into their bodies as he had done to her in this very suite? Her fingers curled into tight little fists. Well, even if he had—that was really none of her concern. His life was not her life, not any more.

Black eyes glanced up to meet hers with a mocking glance, but Emma could detect the darker emotions which lay behind it. Because she wasn't stupid. Or blind. She knew that beneath that ruggedly urbane exterior beat the heart of a primitive Sicilian man, with all the passion and possession which seemed to go along with that.

And because of that, she must tread very carefully. She needed to show him that she was a good mother. She needed to convince him that never again would she attempt to keep Gino from him. She would even eat humble pie if that was what it took to make things better between them. She wasn't going to have unrealistic expectations which could never be met—but surely they could work something out.

His eyes flicked over her from head to toe as he walked back from the bedroom looking all dark and predatory male, and Emma felt suddenly shy. Had she really lived with this man? Shared his bed every night? Now it seemed so long ago that it was like looking at another lifetime—she could barely remember it.

She attempted a smile. 'How do I look?' she said, taking the first tentative step towards a civilised relationship.

How did she look? A pulse beat at Vincenzo's temple. When she smiled like that you could almost forget that she was a lying and deceitful witch. Could almost imagine that she was that same shining blonde angel who had once captivated him. 'Come a little closer so that I can see you properly.'

Feeling a little like a slave who was being brought to stand in front of her master, Emma moved forward a little and gave another smile, more forced this time. 'How's that?'

'Mmm.' He studied her with the objective assessment of a man buying a new car. 'Well, you look a hundred times better than you did ten minutes ago,' he conceded softly. 'I would of course prefer it if you were wearing nothing at all, but it might throw up something of a distraction during dinner. Never mind, there will be plenty of time for that once we've eaten.'

Emma flushed. What a *hateful* way of putting it. As if she were to be served up to him like an after-dinner mint! 'I agreed to accompany you to Sicily,' she said, her voice shaking. 'I don't remember agreeing to anything else.'

'Oh, come on, Emma,' he taunted. 'Let's not pretend any more—what's the point? We've already had a taste of the forbidden and all it has done is awaken our appetite for more. You want me just as much as I want you. I can see it in your eyes, in the way your breasts peak when I look at them, in the way your body reacts to mine even though you're trying your best not to let it show. So why not capitalise on that?'

His words mocked her but that didn't seem to diminish the effect they were having on her. He was right, damn him. Emma suddenly felt as if she were on fire as he pulled her into his arms. She wanted to tell him that she was more than just a responsive body, that she was a woman with feelings and a heart which had been broken once and which she didn't think could bear being broken again. 'But you said…'

'Mmm? What did I say?' he murmured as he pulled her even closer and began to drift his lips along the curve of her jaw.

'I…' His caress was too intoxicating. Emma couldn't remember. Now his hands were on her breasts, playing with them through the expensive silk of her dress, and she felt their arousal pinpoint so exquisitely that it felt almost like pain. 'Vincenzo,' she whispered.

'You like that, don't you?'

'Yes!' The word was torn from her lips as if she had lost control of her speech. Again, it was as if he had cast some powerful spell over her. All she could hear was the thunder of her heart and all she could feel was the soft, insistent aching of desire.

'Ah, Emma,' he said softly as his hand skimmed the slippery surface of her silk-covered bottom. 'How quickly you turn on.'

Only for you, she thought. *Only for you*. Emma closed

her eyes. One second more and it would be too late and he would peel off the dress that she had only just put on. Once more she would become a compliant sex-object, further weakening her bargaining power with a man who used women as puppets and playthings. And Gino had only just gone to sleep! With an effort, Emma pulled away from him, realising with a sudden pang that he hadn't even kissed her. 'Don't,' she whispered.

His eyes narrowed. 'I thought we'd agreed to skip the game-playing.'

'This isn't a game, Vincenzo. Gino's next door, in case you'd forgotten.'

'I am hardly like to forget, am I?' he questioned bitterly.

Abruptly he dropped his hands and moved away from her as he fought the primitive urge to just push her to the ground and take her there and then. And yet, un-expectedly, he found himself surveying her with an element of approval. For wouldn't he have despised her if her cries of pleasure had woken up their baby son? If she had sought her own gratification at the expense of her son then wouldn't she have diminished her worth as a woman, as well as a mother?

'You ought to eat something,' he said suddenly. 'No wonder you're so damned thin—you've barely touched a thing all day. Let's go down for dinner. The hotel is happy to provide us with a trained nanny to babysit while we eat.'

She shook her head. 'I'd rather not leave him, if you don't mind. He might wake up and get scared and it's a brand-new environment and I'd hate him to cry for me and me not be here and I…' Her words ran out along with her breath and she stared up into his impassive face, giving a small shrug of her shoulders. 'I expect you think that sounds ridiculous?'

His eyes narrowed as he hardened his heart to the wide appeal in her blue eyes. 'Actually, I think it sounds admirable—and just the thing to impress the divorce lawyer. Top marks for diligence, Emma.'

'You honestly think…' Emma stared at him '…that's the reason I'm doing it—to earn some kind of Brownie points from a lawyer?'

Vincenzo tried to ignore the wounded look which had clouded those amazing eyes. How dared she look like some innocent young animal who had been unexpectedly felled by an arrow when she had been shallow enough to abandon her marriage at the first opportunity and then to keep his son hidden from him?

And yet Vincenzo had seen the evidence of his own eyes, which had forced him to contradict some of his earlier judgements. She might have brought the child up in relative poverty and she might dress like a pauper herself, but he could see for himself that Gino had been well cared for. He seemed to be a very contented baby and all the money in the world couldn't buy that.

'No,' he conceded heavily. 'I accept that you look after the child well.'

The compliment threw her. It was a capitulation she had not anticipated and Emma blinked, thinking that the

unexpected consideration was almost more painful than
the insults he had hurled her way. Because thoughtful-
ness was too close to kindness and it hinted at times
past, when she had been at the centre of his universe.
She wanted to grip his arms and to demand to know
what had happened to that time and all those feelings,
but she knew deep down that it would be a complete
waste of time.

'In that case, why don't you order something from
room service?' He flicked her a brief, hard smile before
heading off towards the master bedroom. 'While I go
and take a shower.'

Emma walked over to the giant desk, glad to have
something to distract her from the thought of Vincenzo
stripping off naked in the next room—though the menu
slightly threw her, too.

How quickly she had forgotten what it was like to live
the life of a rich woman. It seemed bizarre that a single
dish on this fancy list cost more than her entire food
budget for a week. On a normal day the idea that she
could have carte blanche to select anything that took her
fancy would have filled her with excitement, but this was
not a normal day—not by any stretch of the imagination.

She ordered steak and chips, fresh fruit for pudding
and half a bottle of red wine, and when the two waiters
arrived with the trolley, Vincenzo was just emerging
from the bedroom, dressed in dark trousers and a silk
shirt. Tiny droplets of water, which glittered silver in the
dark hair, gave off an air of intimacy. Why, to an

outsider's eyes they must look like the perfect married couple, she thought wryly

They sat down in silence as silver domes were whipped from meals and the wine opened with flamboyant flourish.

Eventually, the waiters left and when the door had closed behind them Vincenzo frowned as she stared blankly at her plate. 'Just eat something, will you, Emma?' he said impatiently. 'And stop sitting there looking so damned fragile.'

Quickly, she picked up a chip and ate it and the hot salty taste must have awakened her neglected taste buds because she began to eat with genuine hunger, finishing off half her steak before she noticed that Vincenzo was sitting staring at her with a mocking expression on his face, his own meal untouched.

'Better?' he queried sardonically.

'Much better,' she agreed lightly. But even though the food had restored some of her strength, the thoughts which swirled around in her head continued to make her feel uneasy. How strange and yet how familiar it felt to be sitting eating a meal with him like this again. And what on earth was it going to be like returning to Sicily, to the place where she'd first fallen in love with him?

But in a way it was easier to push the questions aside than to seek answers. To revel in this uneasy peace, however brief it might be. To pretend that they really *were* a happily married couple. With, of course, one notable exception. Because if she wanted to keep her heart safe, then she needed to keep her physical distance.

Ostentatiously, she yawned. At least there were lots of bedrooms in this luxurious suite and the beds were bound to be like welcoming havens where she could pull the duvet over her head and blot out the world for the night. 'I think I'll hit the sack,' she said. 'It's been a long day.'

Vincenzo smiled. At times she could be so utterly transparent. 'My very thoughts, *cara*,' he said softly. 'I can think of nothing better than an early night.'

'But…you've hardly eaten anything.'

'I'm not hungry. Well, at least…not for food. Only for you.' He took a slow swallow of red wine and put the glass down before rising to his feet and coming round the table towards her.

Emma's heart was beating fit to burst. 'I'm not going to go to bed with you.'

Softly, he laughed. 'Oh, yes, you damned well are.' He pulled her to her feet as if she were composed of nothing more than feathers and then tipped her face up towards him so that it was fully open to the blazing intensity of his gaze. 'We are going to share a bed as would any married couple if they were here tonight— and you'd better get used to it, Emma, because that's exactly what we shall be doing once we reach Sicily.'

'To save face?' she challenged, and as she saw his face darken she knew that she'd hit on a raw nerve.

'Perhaps there is something in that,' he conceded, in a rare moment of self-scrutiny, but then his mouth curved. 'But mainly because you always did give me the best sex I've ever had, and that much hasn't changed.'

Somehow he managed to make even *that* sound like an insult. 'And if I refuse?'

'You wouldn't dare refuse, even if you wanted to—or had the power to resist me,' he said softly. 'You have far too much to lose.'

Wildly, she shook her blonde head. 'That's sexual blackmail!' she protested.

'On the contrary, Emma,' he demurred as he brought her closer to his hard heat and saw her eyes widen in darkened disbelief and desire. 'I am simply allowing you the opportunity to act like this is nothing to do with you. That this…' and he felt her convulsive tremble as he trickled a fingertip across one very aroused nipple '…is not what you want me to do. I am happy to do that, *cara*, if it helps square it in what passes for your conscience. More than happy.'

And without further ado, he bent and lifted her into his arms, carrying her into the master bedroom, where he peeled from her body the brand-new blue silk dress which she had put on only a couple of hours before.

CHAPTER TEN

'LOOK, Gino, look! Imprint this moment upon your memory for ever, *mio figlio*—for this is the land of your father.'

Vincenzo's voice drifted on the clear air and Emma watched him carrying his son down the steps of the private aircraft, holding him carefully aloft as if he were in possession of a precious trophy. And despite powerful words which she suspected were intended to exclude her, she felt the tug of conflicting emotions at being back on the island she had always loved.

The first time she'd seen Sicily, she had thought it a paradise and one of which its people were passionately and rightly proud. But Vincenzo had been based at the Roman headquarters of the Cardini Corporation and that was where they had been based after their marriage. Yet they had always come here on high days and holidays and so she had seen the land in all its many guises. And the one thing Emma had learnt was that Sicily was a land with many different faces.

Along the coastline glittered lemon and orange or-
chards, which contrasted so beautifully with the dark
green forests of the north-east. At the island's centre was
land and rolling hills, with almond trees and olive
groves and endless fields of wheat. And during the
springtime the wild flowers made a bright rainbow of
colours against the bright green of the fields.

The Cardini family had properties dotted everywhere—
including a winter ski-lodge, where once she had squealed
with excitement to see palm trees dusted with snow.

It was cold now, but the sky was bright blue and the
sun was shining and Emma pulled her pashmina a little
closer as she saw a car waiting for them on the airstrip.

'Is there a car seat for Gino?' she asked.

Black eyes met hers over the top of Gino's hooded
little head. 'Of course there is. I have instructed that
every preparation should be made for his arrival.'

He watched as she put the baby in the car seat and
familiarised herself with the straps, his thoughts for
once not focussed on her bottom or her duplicity, but on
the dramatic change she and the baby had brought to his
life. He had started to realise that with children around,
you could operate on two completely different levels.
There were all the mechanics of looking after a baby and
the small talk which surrounded that—talk which usually bore no resemblance to the thoughts which were
teeming around his head.

As he slid onto the back seat Gino made an affection-
ate lunge at him and Vincenzo's mouth automatically

softened into a smile. It was impossible for your heart not to lift in the presence of such an enchanting baby, he thought—and it brought home to him how much he had already bonded with his son.

He turned to the woman by his side, her blonde hair tied back into a sleek pony-tail, her blue eyes huge in her pale face. In a creamy cashmere coat, she looked expensive and pampered and scarcely recognisable as the waif who had slunk into his office the other day.

'And how are you feeling this morning?' he questioned softly.

Emma was disorientated, that was how she was feeling. And still dazed by the speed at which things seemed to have happened. Were still happening. Feeling displaced in more ways than one, she found herself having to fight against her own instincts. She wanted to reach out to touch Vincenzo's lips, as if to reassure herself that they were the same lips which had grazed over every inch of her body last night at the hotel. Which had whispered to her in soft and sometimes harsh Sicilian words. Which had bitten out a wild cry during his climax so that just for a moment she had felt close to him once more. But it seemed that once the sun had come up, they had became formal strangers again, united only by the child. Reminding her that this was nothing more than an arrangement with a very uncertain outcome.

So stop burying your head in the sand, Emma. Start confronting reality instead of lapsing into the temporary magic of his lovemaking. 'Vincenzo, we need to talk.'

'So talk.'

'We need to discuss what's going to happen once Gino has met your family,' she said, and paused. 'About what we are going to do next.'

He turned to look at her, at the wary look which had clouded her blue eyes. What did she expect him to say in the circumstances? 'Now is not the time, Emma. I haven't decided yet.'

Emma shook her head in frustration. That was Vincenzo all over. That autocratic way he had of just closing off channels of communication and expecting her to go along with it. Well, maybe once she would have done, but not any more. 'But it isn't just *your* decision to make, is it?' she questioned softly. 'I have just as much say in the future as you do.'

Black eyes studied her. 'And how do you see that future?'

For a moment his voice sounded almost *reasonable*. Didn't she dare risk telling him the truth? Was there some corner of his hard heart which might listen to reason? 'I don't know,' she admitted in a strangled voice. 'I mean—I know you're going to want to see Gino and I'm not really in any position to try to stop you—'

'No, you aren't,' he interrupted softly. 'Even though you've done your level best to try.'

The look in his eyes was intimidating but hadn't she vowed that she wasn't going to let him do that any more? 'I just can't bear the thought that he'll spend time away from me. The thought that he'll grow up and

I'll miss something. A word. A smile. A step. Or the fact that he might have a nightmare and call out for me.' Her mouth crumpled with pain. 'And I won't be there,' she said hoarsely.

He leaned forward then, his face savage, and it was as if the man who had brought her such sweet pleasure during the night had been vanquished by this suddenly threatening version of him.

'You don't think it's the same for me?' he ground out. 'You don't think that it might tear me apart to have to let him go now that I have found him at last?'

She wanted to say, *But I'm his mother!* Yet even in her turmoil she knew that this was the wrong thing to say, and not just because Vincenzo would shoot her down in verbal flames. But because she recognised with unwavering certainty that already he would lay down his life for his son.

Once he had declared his love for her with similar passion, but with a man and a woman it was completely different. You loved your child unconditionally but adult love could wither and die.

And suddenly a wave of regret washed over her and she found herself wishing for the impossible. That he still loved her and that they could make it work. 'Don't let's fight,' she whispered. 'Gino doesn't like it.'

Their eyes met for one long moment of silent battle before Vincenzo tore his eyes away from her lips and the urgent desire to kiss them. Instead, he turned his head to look outside the window, at the familiar landscape leading towards the lush countryside where the

Cardini family had been making wines and manufacturing oils for over a century.

As always, the sight of his beloved island set his senses on fire, but today he felt as if they were ablaze and so hot that they were heating his blood to boiling point. It was fatherhood, it was coming home—it was both those things, but it was Emma, too, he realised bitterly. Despite the amazing discovery and distraction of fatherhood, she still intoxicated him like no other. Just as she always had.

And yet their affair should never have come to anything. Time and time again he had told himself that. She should have been just another English girl he'd had a fling with, which should never have lasted beyond the time of her holiday.

Her effect on him had perplexed and captivated him during their strange and fragmented courtship. For the first time in his life Vincenzo had found himself at the mercy of feelings he could not trust and, in the end, his judgement proved to have been flawed. For Emma had been a perfect mistress but a terrible wife. And now? Now she fell into the strange netherworld of being neither.

'At least tell me a little bit about where we're going to be staying?' Emma was asking, her soft voice breaking into his reverie. 'At the vineyard, I suppose?'

Vincenzo shook his head, forcing his mind back to practicalities. 'No, I don't stay there any more. Last year I bought a property a little distance away.'

She didn't realise she had been holding in her breath until it came out in a little hiss of relief. 'Oh.'

'You are pleased?'

Emma shrugged. The situation was difficult enough without an audience watching and analysing their every move. And what a critical audience it was. The Cardini vineyard was a massive, sprawling place with cousins dropping in and out as the fancy chose them. 'It is a bit of a relief,' she admitted. 'I've been dreading living in close proximity to all your relatives, if you must know. They never approved of me.'

'It was our marriage they may have had reservations about. It is strongly engrained in our culture that I should have married a Sicilian girl.'

'So they'll be delighted to have been proved right?'

'I don't think that anyone has ever considered the failure of a marriage any cause for celebration,' he said drily. 'Anyway, most of my cousins have been fixing up deals in North America. Even Salvatore isn't back until next week.'

Emma looked up. 'That long?'

'You sound anxious, Emma,' he murmured sardonically.

She wouldn't have cared if she'd never set eyes on any of his exacting cousins ever again—and Salvatore, the eldest, was the most exacting of all. 'I just wasn't sure…' she shrugged awkwardly '…how long we'd be staying on Sicily for.'

'Well, let me assure you that I wasn't planning on an overnight visit, *cara*,' he drawled.

Her fingers began to pluck at the pashmina around

her neck, aware of Vincenzo showing his authority. 'What have you told everyone about Gino?'

'Just that I will be bringing my son to meet his family.'

She searched his face for clues. 'And how have they taken it? Didn't they ask questions?'

'They would not dare to,' he said softly. 'For that would be an intrusion. I am not seeking anyone's approval or judgement of what has happened, Emma. That is and remains private, just between the two of us.' He leaned forward and spoke rapidly to the driver as the car skirted a medieval headland, which Emma recognised as Trapani. 'Look over there, Emma,' he said. 'And you can see the Egadi Islands.'

Forgetting all the potential pitfalls which awaited her, Emma allowed her gaze to drink in a sea the colour of sapphire. 'It's gorgeous.'

'Do you remember the day we took the boat out?' he questioned, not meaning to.

'And drifted around for hours—' she began, suddenly realising where all this was leading her. Into dangerous waters, that was where.

Their eyes met. Was he recalling how he had taken her into one of the cabins and made love to her and when they'd returned to the deck the sun had been starting to go down in a blaze of fire? But then it had been about *more* than just amazing chemistry between them, a chemistry which undeniably still existed. Back then, they'd been floating along on a bubble of love and just because that bubble had burst it didn't stop it hurting when she let herself think about it.

'Tell me about your house,' she said instead, keeping the shakiness from her voice only with an effort.

An odd kind of smile edged at the corners of his lips. 'Why don't you take a look and see for yourself?' he said softly. 'It's up there.'

A house was obviously completely the wrong way to describe it because the building which swam into Emma's line of vision was in fact an old castle, complete with turrets, huge gates and a fabulous command over the surrounding countryside. The car drew nearer and she could see old stone walls and as they drove into an exquisite old courtyard dotted with palm trees and greenery, Emma swallowed. 'There's a tower,' she said, with a sense of disbelief.

'There are four of them, actually. And a chapel.'

'Mu-mu-mu-mum!' gurgled Gino.

The baby's voice stirred her into action and Emma got out of the car with knees which were curiously wobbly. Her senses shaken by the rush of beauty and the painful stir of emotion, she went round to the other door and began to lift Gino out. He made incomprehensible baby noises, his breath warm against her cheek, and her arms tightened around him. 'See where we are, darling?' she questioned shakily. 'Isn't it beautiful? It's a castle—a real, live castle!'

'Come and take a look at the view from over here,' said Vincenzo.

Trying to tell herself that she *wasn't* asleep, and that

this wasn't some kind of amazing dream from which she would soon waken, Emma followed him across the worn stone and went to stare out over the view of soft green hills and the neat stripes of the vineyard. You could actually *see* the Egadi Islands on the horizon. Further along would be the amazing San Vito beach, where once she'd swum and walked in soft golden sands with Vincenzo all that time ago.

How many of the happy times she seemed to have overlooked, she realised. Had she buried them deep so that they would no longer have the power to hurt her, so deep that she had somehow forgotten that they ever existed? Maybe that was what they meant about memory being selective. But surely it was far safer that way than recalling the heights of happiness she had reached as a new bride. What would that do other than cause pain and regret?

Quickly, she walked to the other side of the courtyard where she could see down on a long rectangle of a swimming pool, set in an orange grove and surrounded by grey stone walls. And as her eyes took it all in, she heard the loud chiming of a bell in the tower.

It was, quite simply, breathtaking—and when she turned back, Emma's eyes were shining. 'Oh, Vincenzo, I'd forgotten just how beautiful it could be.'

Vincenzo surveyed her from between shuttered black lashes. And he had forgotten just how bright and blonde and beautiful *she* could be—with the same clear blue eyes and peachy skin making her look as young and as innocent as when he'd first met her.

'Come and see the inside,' he said, telling himself to ignore the softening of her features and the sparkle in her eyes. Her sudden enthusiasm had happened for a reason and he suspected he knew what that reason was. Had the contrast between the lifestyle she'd had in England hit her hard now that she compared it with *his*? Was the enormity of what she had given up when she'd walked away only just hitting her? 'Follow me,' he clipped out.

Emma felt dazed as she followed Vincenzo through the castle. The interior was cool, with marble floors and dark beamed ceilings—and a series of rooms, each more elegant than the last. Eventually they reached the less formal of two lofty salons and standing there was a middle-aged woman dressed entirely in black, whose face seemed familiar.

'You remember Carmela?' queried Vincenzo.

The woman who had helped his grandmother rear him. Who had been kind to her when she'd returned from England as Vincenzo's bride. 'Yes, of course I do. *Buon giorno, Carmela. Come sta?*' It was worth pulling her very basic Italian out of the memory bank just to see Vincenzo's look of surprise, and the woman in black beamed with pleasure.

'*Bene, bene, Signora Emma.*' Speaking in a rapid stream of the Sicilian dialect, Carmela advanced towards Gino, who was eyeing her with extreme caution.

Each plump baby cheek was squeezed between Carmela's thumb and forefinger amid more exclaiming, to which Vincenzo made a murmured reply and Emma found herself smiling as she looked at him. 'What is she saying?'

'She is telling us that we have the most beautiful son in the world and I thanked her for confirming it. And she also said that her daughter, Rosalia, is coming over later. She has a boy a little older than Gino and she would be honoured to babysit for us any time.'

'I'm not leaving him with anyone he doesn't know,' said Emma quickly.

Vincenzo studied her for a moment. 'Then he will get to know them and soon,' he said, giving her an impenetrable look. 'For I intend that as many people as possible should make the acquaintance of my son and heir.'

His words were unashamedly proprietorial and a flicker of foreboding briefly unsettled her but Emma tried to banish it—telling herself that of course he made the declaration sound almost tribal, because that was the way it was here, in this fiercely proud family of his. And why *shouldn't* Vincenzo show his son off to the others? *Because it excludes me. Leaves me on the periphery, wondering where my place in all this is, and realising that I don't have one.*

But surely those were selfish thoughts, and not in her son's best interests?

'I need to change the baby,' she said.

Vincenzo nodded. She could be stubborn but at least nobody could accuse her of not being a hands-on mother. Because surely that would have been the worst-case scenario—to have an estranged wife who simply didn't care? Even some of his *married* friends in Rome had those kind of wives—ones who seemed happy to delegate all the childcare to some young slip of a thing, while the mothers were more interested in shopping and lunching and flying to Milan to attend the catwalk shows.

'Let me show you the bedrooms,' he said. 'Roberto will have taken the luggage through by now. I thought that the suite at the far end of the castle would be best—then at least you won't have to carry Gino up and down those stairs.'

It was thoughtful of him; she couldn't deny that. The stairs *did* look precarious, all winding and steep like a mountain pass. 'And where are your sleeping quarters?' she questioned.

A smile played around the corners of his mouth. 'Please don't be naïve, Emma,' he murmured. 'As we discussed in London, we shall be sharing a bedroom, of course.'

Her heart missed a beat. 'So you can stay close to your son?'

'Yes, but also,' he whispered softly, 'to give me ample opportunity to enjoy your beautiful body.'

She felt torn between despair at his arrogance and a tearing elation at the thought of spending the night in his arms. As if she could hardly wait to claw at the oiled silk skin which sheathed his powerful and muscular physique. A time when hostilities could be forgotten, blotted out with bliss.

But sex isn't a cure-all, she reminded herself fiercely. *It's a danger and a distraction which can blind you from seeing the truth*. Yet she said nothing as she followed him through the seemingly endless maze of corridors to a sumptuous suite of rooms overlooking the lush and tropical gardens. What would be the point of raising another objection which he would simply shoot down in flames?

All their cases were already there and Emma set about unpacking Gino's, still unused to the range of luxurious new outfits and the sheer volume of choice. She changed his nappy and dressed him in a warm navy blue jump suit with the sweetest little sailor collar. And tiny sheepskin boots! Vincenzo was standing leaning against the window sill, just watching her, saying nothing.

Emma looked down at the floor doubtfully where ancient silken rugs were thrown over the stone flags. 'Will he be all right if I put him down there?' she questioned. 'Or would you like to hold him while I freshen up?'

He felt like saying sarcastically that he didn't actually need her permission to take his son, but was beginning to realise just how much she must have been tied by bringing up a baby, entirely on her own. He remembered his own childhood surrounded by Cardini cousins running in and out of his grandmother's home. There had always been a constant support mechanism for his uncles and aunts, he realised. But for Emma there had been none of that.

'What happens when he starts to crawl?' he questioned.

Emma walked into an exquisite, blue-tiled bathroom, aware that he was following her with Gino in his arms. She filled up a basin with warm water and began to wash her hands with soap which smelt of lime blossom, its suds soft and sensual as she washed away the inevitable grime of the journey.

She spoke to his reflection in the mirror. 'Crawling's when all the fun starts, apparently. He doesn't crawl yet, but the health visitor told me to get into practice so it won't come as a shock when he does.'

'You must never be able to let them out of your sight once they're mobile,' he said slowly.

'No.' Emma pulled the plug and turned round, her hands enveloped in the softest towel she had used in ages, thinking that they sounded like two rational people talking, instead of Emma and Vincenzo with their passion and their fury. 'Unless you put them in a playpen, of course.'

'You don't sound as if you approve of them.'

'Not really, no. They remind me of cages and babies aren't animals. They need the freedom to explore—but sometimes you need to keep them safe while you do something. Even if it's something like going to the bathroom.' Stupidly, she found herself blushing. Wasn't it funny that some things seemed even more intimate than sex? In the past she wouldn't have dared say such a thing to him. 'I'm sorry, I don't know why I told you that.'

But Vincenzo shook his head, filled suddenly with a strange rage—yet more against himself than at anyone else. 'Am I such a tyrant that you would not dare to speak of such things?'

Awkwardly, Emma shrugged.

'Tell me,' he demanded.

She looked into his black eyes. 'You didn't exactly encourage communication when we were married—but maybe that's best. It's the old-fashioned idea, isn't it—that a woman should be shrouded in mystique?'

He noted her use of the past tense. But she was right, wasn't she? The marriage *was* in the past.

'And I was too unsure of myself to know what to say to you,' she admitted. 'How much to confide and how much to keep inside.' She had become aware that she had somehow managed to marry one of Sicily's most eligible men and that discovery had blown some of her confidence away. She had felt too gauche and inexperienced to be able to live up to her new role. Instead of revelling in all the new pleasures and joys of married life, inside she had clammed up with fear. Maybe that was why she hadn't become pregnant.

'You were unhappy in Rome,' he said suddenly.

It sounded more an observation than a question, but he was looking at her as if he required an answer. 'Well, I was a bit lonely,' she admitted. 'Or, rather, I was isolated. I had my Italian lessons, but not a lot else. You were at work all day. And you refused to countenance the idea of me working.'

Vincenzo shook his head impatiently as she brought up the well-worn complaint. 'But you *had* no career,

Emma,' he pointed out acidly. 'You had dropped out of catering school. So what would you have suggested? That I should have my wife—a *Cardini* wife—making *cupcakes*?'

His words were now edged with their familiar sarcasm and Emma looked at him with a steady gaze. Why should she think he'd suddenly become a reasonable man? Why, that would require a personality change so radical that he simply wouldn't be recognisable as Vincenzo at the end of it.

'Oh, forget it. It doesn't matter. And now if you'll excuse me—I need to feed Gino,' she said, in a flat voice.

CHAPTER ELEVEN

IT WAS like being in limbo—that was if such a place could take you from one extreme emotion to the next, often in just a matter of hours. Emma was back in Vincenzo's arms and Vincenzo's bed and to the outside world she was once again Signora Cardini.

Except that she wasn't. Not really. Mostly, it was just an act they were putting on, where occasionally real feelings managed to struggle through the façade to make themselves known. Feelings which were mainly to do with their son and Emma clung on to that fact like a drowning woman scrabbling at a slippery rock. Their fierce love for Gino was the one genuine thing which sustained her, because the other stuff was pure, seductive danger.

How easy it would be to concentrate on the magic of her nights with Vincenzo, when she joined him in the huge bed which dominated the master bedroom of the castle. Where inhibitions had been banished. Where she slipped between crisp, cotton sheets to collide with the

warm power of his naked body as he pulled her against
his wild, seeking heat.

It was as if he was seeking to obliterate the memory
of those last arid months in Rome, where their relationship had deteriorated to such an extent that they had
become like icy strangers to each other. Now he seemed
determined to take her to heights of passion which afterwards left her shaking and confused. Wondering how
she could let herself be so carried away by such a proficient but ultimately emotionless demonstration of his
sexual experience.

And wondering too how much she was going to miss
him when she went back to England.

By day, Vincenzo showed a bemused and fascinated
Gino his beloved island, while Emma reacquainted herself with a beauty she had forgotten—her pleasure
tempered by the pain of remembering snapsnot mo-
ments which seemed to appear from odd corners of her
mind when she was least expecting them.

A stunning view over the stunning coastline of the
tiny island of Ustica, with its inky rocks and arid landscape, became merged with a memory of Vincenzo kissing her, telling her that her hair was like spun gold, only
far more precious.

Why had it changed? Why did relationships change
and then warp so badly that they became unrecognisable
and you could never get the happiness back again? And
why did you never realise the importance of tenderness, until it had gone?

But at least Gino was blossoming, settling into life on Sicily as if he had been born to it. And maybe he had—for that was certainly what Vincenzo seemed to think. 'All Sicilians are tied by the heart to this island,' he told her, in that drawlingly arrogant way of his which broached no argument.

Some days, Carmela's daughter Rosalia brought her own little son, Enrico, to play, and the two sturdy little babies sat opposite each other on a large rug, alternately glowering and giggling at each other.

'Think how it will be when they walk!' said Rosalia, whose English was good.

Emma shot Vincenzo a quick glance. This wasn't a permanent arrangement. He knew that and she knew that—so surely he wasn't allowing everyone else to think otherwise?

But she didn't get a chance to ask him—because Salvatore and the rest of the Cardini cousins had unexpectedly flown in a day early and a large party was being arranged at the vineyard so that they and the rest of the family could meet Gino formally at last.

'What on earth am I going to wear?' questioned Emma edgily, her nerves getting the better of her. Gino had been sick on the white woollen baby suit she had been saving ever since Rosalia had told her that Cardini children always wore white for celebrations. It was the most impractical thing she'd ever heard, thought Emma crossly—pulling down another pristine little snow-coloured top over his dark, silky curls.

'For a woman who looks best in nothing at all, it's a bit of a dilemma,' Vincenzo murmured.

Emma shot him a glance, thinking how unusually satisfied he sounded. Like a lion in the jungle who had just eaten a large meal, its predatory nature quietened for a while so that you could almost be fooled into thinking it would be okay to stroke it. But, in effect, wasn't that exactly what had just happened?

Gino had spent the morning playing at Enrico's house and Vincenzo had rushed her straight back here to 'make the most of our free time, *cara*' as he had put it. This could have been translated into any language as him carrying her straight into their bedroom where he had proceeded to undress her and take her to bed. Which explained her high colour, which wouldn't seem to go away, or the fact that her heart was still pounding wildly with the memory of all the things he had done to her....

She looked up to realise that he was talking to her. 'What?'

'I said, do you want me to take over dressing Gino while you get changed?'

Emma nodded. 'Yes, please.'

She went into the dressing room and began to search through the hangers. What to wear in a situation like this was inevitably going to be a minefield, made worse by the critical presence of the chauvinistic Cardini men.

She ran her fingers along the row of clothes. Nothing too low, too short, too clingy or too revealing. And it was an afternoon/early evening party to accommodate all the young Cardini children who would be there, so it couldn't be too dressy, either.

In the end, she chose a simple cream cashmere dress, buckled a soft leather belt around the waist and pulled on a pair of matching boots.

She walked out into the sitting room where they were waiting for her, and just for one moment Emma's heart missed a beat. Gino looked so *perfect* and he seemed so perfectly happy, too, as he nestled in the arms of his father, swiping little baby punches at his autocratic chin. Like the textbook father and son, they could have been used in an advertising campaign to represent masculine bonding.

And nothing is really as it seems, she reminded herself painfully. *Life, just like adverts, can be nothing but an illusion.*

'Are you teaching him how to fight?' she questioned reprovingly.

Black eyes were flicking over her. From the soft swell of her breasts to the indentation of her tiny waist and the slender curve of her hips, which was accentuated by the fine wool.

'Mmm?'

She wished he wouldn't look at her like that. It made her heart flutter. It made her body ache. And it made her heart yearn for what could never be. 'I *said*, are you teaching him how to fight?'

He smiled as he dodged another mock-punch from Gino's pudgy fist. *'Sì, cara mia,'* he murmured. 'All men need to know how to fight.'

She knew that it was pointless to protest that Gino wasn't yet a year old, just as she knew it was pointless to tell him to wipe that mocking look off his face. As if he was determined to taunt her with the slow smoulder of his eyes and his lazy scrutiny of her body.

Her fingertips fluttered anxiously to the buckle of her belt. 'Do I look okay?'

'You know you look utterly delectable. The mirror does not lie, Emma.'

She sighed and picked up her handbag. 'You don't get it, do you, Vincenzo? Women aren't seeking affirmation when they ask a question like that—they're seeking reassurance and it's usually because they're nervous. I just want to know if you think I am suitably dressed for a large Cardini gathering.'

He gave a slow smile. '*Indubbiamente,*' he murmured.

'What does that mean?'

'Undoubtedly.'

'Useful piece of vocabulary—I'll use it next time I'm in a shop,' she said.

'Or use it tonight in bed, when I ask if I have pleased you,' he murmured.

'As if you ever have to ask!'

'There *is* that,' he admitted, with unashamed arrogance and Emma had to turn away quickly.

This is getting too complicated, she thought as their words mimicked an easy intimacy. *It's starting to feel like something it can never be and you're going to get hurt if you're not careful.*

Vincenzo saw the sudden set of her shoulders as she turned away and his eyes hardened. Why had he allowed himself to forget that she was simply here on sufferance? Because her beauty had blinded him, that was why—just as it had always blinded him. He picked Gino up. 'Let's go,' he said roughly.

He drove them there himself and Emma's mouth was dry with nerves as the car bumped its way over the dusty track leading to the vineyard. It was a long time since she'd been here—to the beautiful estate which was centre of the Cardini industry. She had once asked Vincenzo why the road leading to the lavish home was so basic, and she had never forgotten his reply.

'Because we Sicilians do not flaunt our wealth,' he had said. 'We do not need to, for it is irrelevant. A man is still a man whether he owns a hut or a castle.'

It had gone some way towards explaining the complexity which lay at the heart of the Sicilian people and Emma had been intrigued by it. She had wanted to learn more. To begin to understand the people, and in so doing to maybe further understand the dark and complicated man she had married. But Vincenzo had thwarted all her efforts to delve beneath the surface. She had discovered that beneath his stony exterior lay yet more stone.

She glanced now at his hard, dark profile as he eased his foot off the accelerator and they drove into the huge courtyard, where cars were crowded in, side by side. 'Oh, heavens—it's *huge*!' exclaimed Emma. 'A full-blown family gathering!'

'But of course,' agreed Vincenzo. 'Everyone is here to meet Gino.'

Gino. Silently, Emma realised that what was on offer here was so much more than he would ever have in England. And it wasn't just about wealth, she recognised. Here there were family. People who cared and who would love him with a fierce and unbreakable bond. If anything ever happened to her, Gino would be safe.

'Why didn't we start our married life here, in Sicily?' she questioned suddenly.

His eyes narrowed. 'Because my work was in Rome.'

'But—'

'Yes. I know. I could have worked anywhere.' Vincenzo put his hands on the steering wheel as if he were still driving, even though the engine was no longer running.

He did not find it easy to express his feelings; he never had. As a child there had been no mother to coax from him his anxieties and his fears and although his beloved grandmother had loved him fiercely, she had been a member of the old school. Where men were strong and never gave anything away and only women showed their emotions.

He wasn't finding it particularly easy now, but Emma was looking at him expectantly. 'I guess I thought that you would find the island too small and too claustrophobic,' he said slowly. 'That Rome might be a more compatible lifestyle for a young woman leaving England.'

But Rome had seemed too big. To busy. The rapid

and sophisticated chatter of the Romans had dazzled and confused her, so that Emma had retreated inside herself, feeling isolated on all sides and growing further away from her husband.

Emma stared straight ahead. 'Anyway, none of that matters now, does it? Not really. It's the present we have to deal with.'

There was a fractured kind of pause.

'Let's go inside,' he said, his voice distorted with something like regret as he lifted Gino from the baby-seat and handed him to her.

But Emma lifted her face to his and for once she allowed her composure to slip. 'Vincenzo, I'm scared,' she whispered.

He looked down at her as she caught the baby close to her breast and the breath caught in the back of his throat. And at that moment he wanted...wanted...

The shutters came down again. 'There is no need to be,' he said unevenly. 'They're family.'

Yes, your family, she thought with a slight feeling of desperation. *And Gino's. But not mine. Certainly not mine.*

A murmur of excitement went up as they walked into the hallway and it seemed to Emma that about a hundred little girls of varying ages, all wearing pristine white frocks with different coloured sashes, came squealing out, closely followed by lots of dark, solemn-eyed little boys.

'Oh, my word,' murmured Emma as Gino clung to her neck like a little boa constrictor and screamed out his delight at all the attention he was getting.

There was a blur of introductions to Bellas and Rosas and Marias and Sergios, Tomassos and Pietros. After she'd said *ciao* to each and every one of them, Emma followed Vincenzo into the formal salon—aware that some of the women were looking at her with narrow-eyed suspicion. And if she was being entirely honest, could she really blame them? Wouldn't she have felt exactly the same if the positions had been reversed? They didn't know the whys and wherefores of the marriage breakdown or Gino's conception, because Vincenzo hadn't told them.

It would have been so easy to have blackened her name, her character and her morals, but he had not done so and Emma knew why. Because he was a proud man and pride would not let him. But in so doing, he had protected her, hadn't he?

She thought how ravishingly handsome he looked as he began to reacquaint her with faces from the past and introduce her to new ones.

'But here is someone who needs no introduction.'

Emma kept one hand firmly around Gino's back as she turned to greet the man who stood behind them.

Salvatore Cardini. One scant year older than Vincenzo. Two men who were closer than brothers and yet further apart than brothers could ever be. Theirs was a unique relationship. She remembered being told that Salvatore's mother had wanted to take Vincenzo in, to bring up the orphaned child as one of her own. But the boys' grandmother had been so heartbroken at the death of her daughter that caring for the infant son had been the only light on her inconsolable horizon.

So Vincenzo had been based with Nonna but had spent a lot of time at Salvatore's house. They had walked to school together. Learned to ride and shoot together. To swim and to fish, and then—when they had first reached a manhood which had captivated every female who came within their radar—to seduce any woman who had allowed herself to be seduced.

They looked startlingly similar, with their hard, proud features, haughty demeanour and amazing physiques— but Emma had never seen Salvatore's soft side. She'd always thought that maybe he didn't have one, but right now his face was more meditative than she remembered.

'*Ciao*, Emma,' he said slowly. 'You are looking well.'

She wondered how he might have phrased it if she'd turned up in her normal wardrobe instead of being kitted out by her estranged husband first. Whether he would have been quite so complimentary then! But she leaned forward to accept a kiss on each cheek, aware that Vincenzo had walked over to the other side of the room, leaving them alone together. Like throwing her to the lions, she thought.

'*Ciao*, Salvatore,' she echoed. 'You're looking well yourself.'

He allowed a rare smile, but he was looking at Gino now, fixing him with a piercing gaze as if he were stamping the image of the baby in his mind. And then he nodded. 'But he is the image of Vincenzo,' he breathed softly.

'Yes.' Had he doubted that Vincenzo was the father? she wondered. Of course he had—and who could blame him for doing that? 'Yes, he is.'

Salvatore now directed the gaze at her. 'So how have you been keeping?'

'Oh, you know. We've survived,' she said lightly.

'Yes, I can see that. But life should be about more than survival.' There was a pause. 'Vincenzo tells me that you are a good mother.'

To someone unused to the ways of Sicilian men this might have sounded patronizing, but Emma correctly read it as a huge compliment. She nodded, aware of a sudden deep pang of sadness. 'I hope so. It isn't difficult—he's such a wonderful little boy.'

'But he likes Sicily. He is at home here.'

There was an unmistakable undercurrent to his words. The dark, implicit threat which lay behind the social niceties. 'Who wouldn't like it?' she questioned evenly, but inside her heart was beating furiously with fear. Did he consider Gino to be like a pawn in a chess game—who could be moved around according to the game-plan of the Cardinis?

Vincenzo came back then and she was taken over to sit with some of the older women, where they were served coffee and some of the tiny cakes topped with *frutta martorana*—marzipan shaped and coloured to look like miniature pieces of fruit. But Salvatore's words kept echoing round and round in her head and Emma couldn't concentrate on food. She crumbled most of the sweet delicacy onto her plate—each morsel tasting like cardboard in a mouth grown as dry as parchment.

They didn't leave until gone seven, with all the Cardinis clustered on the doorstep waving them away, and Emma knew that the afternoon had been judged a success. But inside she felt unsettled—like a pack of cards which had been unshuffled. She no longer knew her place.

Yes, in a way this *was* a perfect kind of limbo, but none of it was real. She *knew* the reason she was here. The *only* reason she was here. Because of Gino. Take an unplanned and miraculous baby out of the equation and all you were left with was a man who was still enamoured of her body and a woman…

In the dim shadows of the car she shot him a glance. A woman who remained completely vulnerable to the love she'd once had for him. So what the hell was she going to do about it?

In the darkness, Vincenzo read the unmistakable tension in her body and his mouth tightened, knowing that he could put off the inevitable no longer.

He waited until Gino was asleep and they were sitting at the dining-room table with Emma's meal lying untouched before her, just as she had refused to eat at the party earlier.

A nerve flickered angrily at his temple. Was she hoping that he would read the signals she was sending out without having to say anything? Did she think he was blind? That he was impervious to her restlessness and desire to go home. And didn't she realise that such a scenario would never be allowed to happen?

'Emma. I believe there are matters we need to discuss, don't you?'

She lifted her head slowly, wanting to read something of his intentions in his face, but his features remained as closed as they had ever been. 'About?'

Against the crisp white linen tablecloth his olive fingers flexed and unflexed. So they were back to playing games, were they? Maybe they should talk about it when she was naked and pinned beneath him and begging him to do it to her some more. She was much more amenable *then*, wasn't she? 'About the future, of course.'

'Gino's future?'

'No, not just Gino's. Yours. And mine.'

If only his eyes were not as forbidding as his voice, it might almost have masqueraded as some kind of romantic proposition. But as it was, Emma's heart missed a beat. 'Go on,' she said tightly, her chest tight with fear at what might be coming next. 'I'm assuming you've got some ideas about how you wish to proceed.'

How cold she sounded! he thought. Less like a woman and more like a sulky robot or a trainee lawyer! Well, she had better learn that all the sulking in the world would not change his mind.

He fixed her in the fierce light of his eyes. 'I want Gino to live here in Sicily, Emma. You have to realise that under no circumstances will I allow him to go back to England with you, and what is more—I will not give you the divorce you crave.'

CHAPTER TWELVE

EMMA stared at Vincenzo, her lips trembling with horror, shaken to the core by his words—by their harsh tone as much as their content. And by the cold glint in his black eyes. 'But you said…or, rather, you intimated that this was just going to be a *short* trip to introduce Gino to Sicily and to your relatives!'

He gave a short laugh. 'And were you foolish enough to believe that?' he mocked. 'Did you really think that once I had given my son a taste of what is truly his—his heritage and his future—I would ever allow him to go back to the kind of life you had before?'

Emma shrank back as if he had hit her. 'So you…you *tricked* me,' she accused hoarsely. 'You…you made it sound like a temporary holiday and now you're effectively telling me that I'm a prisoner here on the island? Well, you may be rich and you may be powerful, Vincenzo— but this is the twenty-first century and life doesn't work like that. You can't keep me here against my will.'

'Just try me,' he challenged softly.

Some warning bell sounded loudly in her subconscious as she registered the simmering anger in his body, like some fierce and angry predator about to strike. With an effort, Emma sucked in a shuddering breath. She was going about this the wrong way. *Calm things down.* She tried a weak representation of a smile. 'Look, Vincenzo, let's be reasonable. You can't do this—'

'Oh, but I can and I will, Emma,' he interrupted implacably. 'Unless you are prepared to consider the alternative.'

'Alternative?' She stared at him suspiciously, like a drowning person who had just been thrown a life-raft, only to discover it full of holes. 'What alternative?'

Dispassionately, he studied the pale oval of her face. The bright blue beauty of her eyes. 'That we remain here. Together. As a married couple, bringing up Gino and any other children we may be blessed with.'

It sounded like a cruel joke, but she could see from the look of intent on his arrogant face that he was deadly serious. And yet his words sounded so utterly cold... 'Why would you want to do that?' she whispered.

'Isn't it obvious? You must know that I would never be content playing the role of part-time father. Just as you must know that I would never tolerate the idea of another man bringing up my son, or having any real or lasting influence in his life.' He saw her mouth crumple but he steeled himself against its soft appeal, reminding himself instead of the natural consequences of her beauty.

'And, yes, before you tell me that there *is* no other man, maybe there isn't. At least, not at the moment,' he continued as little darts of jealousy began pricking at his skin. 'But one day there will be, and that much is as clear as night following day. A woman as beautiful as you is not destined to remain alone for long, Emma.'

Oddly enough, this hurt almost as much as anything else. She wanted to tell him that he was a stupid, dense man if he thought that she could ever even *look* at another man after him. But surely that would only pander to an ego which needed no bolstering? And Vincenzo was in no mood to believe her anyway.

'You're barbaric,' she husked, scraping the chair back against the floor as she stood up to face him.

'Am I?' He smiled as he rose to his feet and walked round the table towards her. 'But that seems to be what turns you on, isn't it, Emma?' he boasted softly. 'Maybe it's time you learned to embrace barbarism instead of pretending that it appals you.'

Her breath was coming in short, sharp bursts as she stared at him, shattered by the things he had said and his vision of the future. 'Stay away from me!'

'Say it like you mean it, and I might listen,' he taunted silkily as he pulled her into his arms. 'Though on second thoughts...'

Emma struggled, but only for a moment for his touch was like lighting a match to a piece of tinder. She seemed to have no control over her reaction to him, even though she gave a little moan of protest when he bent his head to graze his lips over hers.

His breath was warm against her mouth, his proximity

intoxicating. 'Why don't you think about my suggestion, Emma? Would it be so bad to live like this, mmm?'

This? But what was this, other than a wild and undeniable chemical attraction? Emma closed her eyes, not wanting him to read the hunger which must be written in them and yet still not strong enough to push him away, despite the fact that he was treating her like an object. A possession. Just the way he always had done.

Even if she did protest—what good would it do? For he would only use his sexual power to kiss her into a kind of melting and mindless submission. 'Vincenzo—'

'Think about it,' he urged huskily. 'We are good together. Many couples do not have what we have.'

'Other couples have compatibility!'

'Compatibility exists when we aren't trying to score points off one another.'

And other couples had love, of course. But she couldn't hope to expect that, not now.

'Do I have a choice?' she whispered, opening her eyes at last to look into the hard, shadowed face and the ebony gaze which lanced into her. 'No, of course I don't. You ride roughshod over everything, Vincenzo. You always did.'

'Yes, you have a choice about how you choose to live your life,' he argued. 'You can act as if you're here under duress, playing the victim-prisoner.' Reflectively, he lifted his hand to drift his fingertips in a soft, curving arc around her jaw. 'Or you can make the best of what we have. Gino. Health. Family. And enough money for life not to be a struggle.'

It was a disingenuous way to describe the vast Cardini fortune and the prospect of a loveless marriage—because when it boiled down to it she *didn't* have any options. How could she, broke and with no prospect of a career, possibly fight the might of Vincenzo Cardini?

Emma felt as if he had thought it all out and was presenting it as a *fait accompli*, while she had nothing to offer in the way of reasonable argument. And even if she had—even if by some remarkable fluke she succeeded in leaving—would Gino ever forgive her if she tried to take him away from all this? Would he one day look back and despise her for having put her own selfish wishes before his welfare?

She pulled away from him—away from the temptation of his touch which seemed capable of making her do things she had no wish to do. 'I can't think about it tonight,' she said, with a weariness which seemed to have penetrated her bones. 'It's been an exhausting day.'

'Then let's go to bed.'

'I don't want to go to bed with you.'

His lips curved into a mocking smile. 'Oh, but I think you do.'

In the circumstances she shouldn't have wanted him. Shouldn't have let him make love to her after issuing such a stark ultimatum. But she did. Heaven forgive her, but she did.

They had barely even shut the bedroom door behind them before he pushed her to the floor and took her with a hunger which she despised herself for matching, tugging urgently at the belt of his trousers as he peeled off her panties, choking out her pleasured shock as he entered her. Even her orgasm felt like a betrayal—her greedy body overriding something she felt instinctively was wrong. Because surely to settle for something as basic as this made a complete mockery of marriage?

Afterwards, they crawled into bed but Emma couldn't sleep. She lay awake until just before dawn, fretting as her heart banged painfully against her breast while the Sicilian slept beside her.

Deliberately, she rolled as far as she could from his body and the false comfort it offered. His proximity was dangerous—his warm heat lulled her into thinking that here she was safe, and she most definitely was not. Emotionally, she couldn't have been in a more perilous place than locked in this loveless marriage for the sake of their son.

In the quietness of the night she felt a tear begin to trickle from behind her tightly shut eyes and she rose before her husband was awake, dressing with a swift determination that he would not see her vulnerable. He might have tricked her into coming here and he might now be using all his power and his might in order to make her remain here as his wife, but she would protect herself. She would make sure that her heart did not get broken again, ruthlessly trampled on by a man who did not love her.

By the time Vincenzo emerged, yawning and stretching his arms like a well-fed cat, Emma was already in the salon, playing with Gino. The tall Sicilian paused by the door and she saw his black eyes narrow in question when he saw her sitting at the table, an empty coffee cup beside her.

'*Buon giorno, bella,*' he murmured.

'Hello.'

His gaze flickered over her face, so pale this morning and with dark circles shadowing her beautiful eyes. He saw the silken tumble of her blonde hair and felt the kick of lust at his groin. 'You are up early,' he observed softly.

She steeled herself against the rugged beauty of his face, but it was made easier by remembering his harsh ultimatum, his insistence that she stay here as his captive wife. 'Perhaps I should have run it past you first?' she questioned coolly. 'You'll have to tell me about that kind of thing—what is and what isn't expected of me—since I'm not exactly sure what your house rules are, Vincenzo.'

His mouth hardened. So this was to be the way forward, was it? Did she think she would break his resolve by adopting the look of an ice-maiden? By behaving as if she had frost in her veins? Well, she would soon discover that he would not be broken. 'You are not in prison!' he pointed out with icy chill.

'No, of course I'm not.' She gave him a serene smile. 'I'm here entirely under my own free will.'

'And now you are deliberately twisting everything I say!'

Emma shook her head and placed a silent finger over

her lips, aware that Gino was watching them, his dark eyes switching from one parent to another as each spoke, like a tiny spectator at a tennis match.

'On the contrary, Vincenzo—I'm telling it exactly as it is. We both know why I'm here—because of our son—and so it's going to be pretty pointless if we then spoil it all by arguing in front of him. If you are determined that we're going to make him a family home here, then at least let's try and make it as non-confrontational as possible.' *If we can't have love, then surely we can learn to enjoy a type of harmony.*

'Emma—'

'Here, you take Gino.' Fixing a bright smile to her lips, she stood up and, depositing a quick kiss on Gino's chubby little neck, she handed him to Vincenzo. 'I'll go and get showered and changed. Did you have any particular plans for the day? No? Then I thought we could go into Trapani.' The words came tumbling out, as if she was using them to try to fill the aching space which lay between them. 'Take Gino in his buggy around the town and maybe have some lunch overlooking the sea. And then we can see about getting me some driving lessons.'

'*Driving* lessons?'

Emma adopted the look of a teacher who had just discovered that her prize pupil had failed the most elemental of spelling tests. 'Yes, of course. I'm going to need to learn how to drive, aren't I? To be able to get around the island when you aren't here.'

'But I will allocate to you a driver! Someone experienced who will be on hand whenever you wish. You know that.'

Emma shook her head. 'But I'm afraid that won't be good enough. I want *some* independence, Vincenzo,' she returned, and gave him a steady look. 'At least allow me that.'

Vincenzo frowned. He couldn't fault her logic and yet such logic unsettled him. He was used to passion when dealing with women—and with Emma more than most. She had been passionate last night when he had taken her—more than passionate; she had blown him away with her response to him. But this morning it was all so different. He felt as if he were dealing with a mannequin instead of a flesh and blood woman who had come to life so beautifully in his arms.

Yet how could he voice his displeasure at such an unsatisfactory state of affairs? He was restricted by the physical presence of his warm and vocal little son, and by his wife's rather stern directive that they should not argue in front of him. And she was right. Of course she was right. He had never felt quite so wrong-footed in his life.

Damn her!

'Very well,' he growled. 'I will speak to someone about teaching you to drive.'

She inclined her head in subordination. *'Grazie.'*

His mouth tightened. *'Prego.'*

But, in a way, Emma discovered that her determination not to let her defences down had became her saviour. Because it was almost easier to play the part of the precision wife than to simply be herself—that weak woman who still loved him. At least she now had a properly defined role with boundaries she could observe.

Somehow it was easier to keep her feelings for Vincenzo in check when she didn't allow them to surface at all. It was as if she had buried them all deep inside her, locked them away so they wouldn't trouble her and make her foolishly yearn to have them fulfilled. Wasn't it easier to retreat, to shut down and behave with the kind of politeness you might display towards a rather formidable flatmate, than to face up to the fact that you had nothing but a shadowy and meaningless marriage?

Only in bed did her façade slip. Only then could she give into what she most wanted to do—which was to cover every silken inch of Vincenzo's glowing olive skin with tiny butterfly kisses which made him moan. Somehow she managed to stifle her own cries of longing and love and to replace them with the shuddering sighs of pleasure which were never far from her lips.

And in the morning she always woke early, slipping silently from their bed before Vincenzo awoke, aware that it was harder to hide emotions in the stark morning light as she hurried in to check on Gino. Sometimes she would clutch her son so tightly, closing her eyes against the tousled dark silk of his curls as she wondered how this strange relationship was going to affect this beautiful child of theirs.

Then the new day would begin and the charade would start all over again. Outwardly perfect but inwardly disturbing. In a way, it was all too easy to step back and to view the two of them as others must see them. Two parents who loved their little boy, but who were poles apart.

But nobody knew the true dynamic of their relationship and, even if they had, no one would have tried to change it or to interfere. The local girls would not have dreamed of trying to snare away a married man and everyone else valued the Cardini connection far too much to ever want to rock the marital boat.

Invitations began to arrive—with people eager to meet Vincenzo's wife—and Emma knew that she was going to have to make herself learn the language if ever she was to integrate properly.

She spoke to Vincenzo about it one morning. They were breakfasting alone, since Gino had slept late—and when their son wasn't there, it sometimes made the tension between them much more tangible. He was their reason for being together…take Gino away and all you were left with was a vacuum.

Emma watched as Vincenzo sliced a pear in half and began to peel it. Those same fingers had slid so deliciously over her skin during the night, but in the cold light of day those intimacies seemed as if they had happened to someone else.

His dark face was shuttered and she thought that his proud mouth was curved into a faint look of disdain. Perhaps Vincenzo was tiring of this arrangement now that he'd had a chance to live it for a while and maybe

he was having second thoughts about keeping his un-
loved wife here. But Emma had been thinking about
how to make the situation more tolerable.

'I ought to learn the Sicilian dialect,' she said as the
curl of fruit rind began to coil like a snake onto his plate.

His dark head jerked up. 'Ought?' he demanded,
seizing on the lacklustre word as if it were an insult to
his language.

Emma shrugged. Sometimes it felt as if she was just
going through the mechanics of living and she suspected that today was going to be one of those days—
when playing the part which had been assigned to her
seemed like a hell of a lot of work. 'It will be a challenge,' she said. 'Both necessary and rewarding.'

Her dutiful words fell like dull blows to his head and
suddenly Vincenzo felt like a man waking slowly from
a dream—or some kind of drug-induced coma. He
blinked as he stared at the woman who sat before him,
her beautiful blue eyes dull, her wide mouth showing
not the faintest tilt of a smile, and a thousand tiny darts
of realisation pricked over his skin. He couldn't bear
this; he couldn't bear the fact that he was responsible
for what Emma had become.

The silver knife clattered to his plate; the fruit forgotten as he pushed it away. 'You don't have to learn to
drive,' he said. 'Nor to speak the dialect, unless of course
it's for Gino's sake—because naturally I intend that he
should be fluent.'

Emma stared at him, stupidly aware that the flesh of

his pear was quickly turning brown. 'I don't know what you're talking about.'

'Don't you?' He gave a mirthless smile. 'You can leave, Emma. Any time you like. You've won. You can go just as soon as you want.'

'G-go? You mean—'

'Leave Sicily.'

Her fist flew to her mouth. 'I'm not leaving Gino behind!'

Vincenzo's face hardened. 'I'm not asking you to,' he said, even though his heart felt as if it were going to split in two at the thought of having to say goodbye to his beloved little boy. 'You can take Gino with you,' he said raggedly. 'All I ask is that you allow me to see him as often as possible. That you let him come here to know, not just his father, but the Sicilian way of life.'

Emma's eyes narrowed. 'You're trying to trick me, aren't you?' she whispered.

'Trick you?'

She nodded, her heart beating wildly with fear. 'I know what'll happen. I'll let him come back for a holiday and you'll snatch him. You'll keep him here and I will be powerless to get him back—unable to fight the might of the Cardini family. That's what you're planning, isn't it, Vincenzo?'

There was a long, fractured pause and when Vincenzo spoke he felt as if every word were a stone. 'You really think I am capable of such a thing?' he questioned heavily.

Emma opened her mouth but something made her shut it again, knowing that the question was far too important for an instinctive, snapped response. She thought of how much Vincenzo adored his little boy with that fierce and yet tender paternal love which lay at the heart of the most macho Sicilian. And she thought of how much love Gino had to give—to both his parents. She imagined the little boy's tears and confusion and heartbreak if he was denied access to his mother, and deep down she knew that Vincenzo simply would not be capable of hurting his son in such a way.

She shook her head. 'No. No, I don't. It was a stupid, thoughtless thing to say and I said it in anger. I'm sorry.'

In a way, her sweet contrition in the face of all that he had thrown at her made it a million times worse—if that were possible—and Vincenzo felt as if someone were stabbing at his heart with a razor blade. 'Please don't apologise, Emma,' he said bitterly. 'Just tell me when you wish to leave and I will fix it.'

She stared at him. When she *wished* to leave? Did he think that she was like some little girl, with her own tame fairy godmother to grant her *wishes*? Remembering her vow not to show vulnerability, to be able to at least walk away with her pride intact, Emma rose from the table and went over to the window.

Through a wobbly blur of tears she stared out at the layered green beauty of the landscape and swallowed. 'I guess I'd better go as soon as possible.' Because surely that would minimise the terrible pain? A short, swift departure must be easier for them all, than a protracted farewell? 'If that's what you want,' she added woodenly.

For a moment Vincenzo felt the savage twist of dark and writhing emotions—feelings which he had spent a lifetime hiding from, the way he'd learnt to hide from the dark pain of his parents' deaths. And for a moment he thought of the easier, softer way which lay there for him to grasp. To tell her yes, *yes*—just go and go now. To get out of his life and leave him in peace—away from this searing pain and these terrible raw feelings.

But something in the resigned set of her narrow shoulders made him flinch. He could see the tremble that she was trying to supress and suddenly something much stronger than a desire to escape began to overwhelm him. It was like a slow bonfire which had been quietly smouldering away—as the feelings he had dampened down for so long, suddenly erupted into wild life.

'No, of course it isn't what I want!' he bit out. 'You really think I want you to go, Emma?'

'I know you don't want Gino to go.' She spoke the words very carefully, just so that there could be no possible misunderstanding.

'You,' he said urgently, and for the first time in his adult life his voice threatened to crack. '*Che Dio mi aiuti!* I don't want *you* to go!'

Emma turned and stared at him, clutching at the window sill, afraid that her knees would buckle and she would fall in some pathetic heap at his feet and all because she had got her wires crossed and misunderstood him. He was talking about Gino. About their son. 'I won't deny you access,' she breathed.

But Vincenzo was empowered by emotion now, overtaken by a hot heat and an urgent desire to tell her the things which had been staring him in the face for so long, only he had been too blind to see them. He crossed the room and took her in his arms, but she was like a lifeless puppet as she stared up at him, all the light gone from her eyes.

'This has nothing to do with Gino!' he declared. 'Not any more. It is to do with you. And with me. With my love for you, Emma—because I love you.'

She shook her head as salt tears began to well up in her eyes. He was mocking her. Taunting her with what might have been. 'No—'

'*Sì!* Heaven help me for taking so damned long to realise it—but I love you. The woman I married. Who captured my heart. Who bore my child and proved to be the finest mother in the world. The woman I never want to lose. The woman I will not lose!' he added fiercely. 'So long as there is air in my lungs and a heart which beats!' He stared at her. 'But can you love me, too? Or is it too late, Emma?'

The pause which followed his question seemed like a million years and yet it was over in the space of a heartbeat. She shook her head. 'No, of course it's not too late,' she whispered. 'I never stopped loving you, Vincenzo—God only knows I've tried often enough.'

The tears were streaming down her face now, threatening to choke her, and Emma reached out for him, touching her fingers to his face as if he were not quite real. As if Vincenzo could not be saying these things, or looking at her in a way she had almost forgotten.

But he was. Everything she had ever wanted was written there on the dark features of the man she loved, though it took a few seconds more before she dared allow herself to really believe it.

''Cenzo!' she sobbed.

'Shh.' He gathered her into his arms and cradled her close to his heart until her trembling and tears subsided. It was possibly the most innocent embrace that Vincenzo Cardini had ever had with a woman and yet without a doubt it was the most potent of all—as the intensity of his emotions rocked the very foundations of his world.

They stood there for a long time—until all the fraught fight had melted away—and Emma gave a soft, shuddering sigh against his neck. And as he tipped her face upwards Vincenzo wiped away the last tear which lingered on the soft rose flush of her cheeks and silently vowed that he would never make her cry again.

She bit her lip, knowing that there were still things she needed to say to him in order to put the past to rest. 'I should never have run away from Rome,' she whispered. 'When things started going wrong in our marriage, I should have stayed and tried to work it out. I should have talked to you about it. I've been a terrible wife.'

He touched his lips to her nose in the most tender of

kisses. 'And maybe you wouldn't have been had I not stepped back by two centuries once I had married you,' he said softly. 'I was a bad husband, Emma. So you see, *cara mia*—we're equal.'

It was something Emma had never thought to hear from her macho, magnificent Sicilian. And even though she thrilled to his admission, there was another, elemental side to her which was contrary enough to fight against such a claim. 'Does that mean you won't ever again expect me to submit to your will?' she questioned innocently.

Vincenzo read the expression in her eyes perfectly and smiled, lacing his fingers with hers as he began to lead her towards the bedroom. 'Interesting question,' he mused softly, his thumb tracing a provocative circle over her palm. 'Why don't we go into the bedroom before our son wakes and discuss it properly, *bella*?'

EPILOGUE

AS PARTIES went it was meant to be a simple occasion—
a large family lunch to say goodbye to Salvatore. But
for Emma it was important and significant—because it
was the first party that she and Vincenzo had ever
thrown as a married couple. She had fussed around in
the preceding week—making sure that the menu would
satisfy everyone and that there would be enough fresh
flowers to adorn the long trestle-tables which were laid
outside, beneath the trees.

Salvatore was leaving the vineyard and Vincenzo
was going to take over the running of it. Sicily was to
be their family home from now on. Where Gino would
thrive and God willing, they would fill their castle with
brothers and sisters for him.

'Why exactly is Salvatore going?' she asked him,
giving one final twirl in front of the mirror and hoping
that the green silk dress didn't look too dressy for a
lunchtime party.

Vincenzo shrugged and gave her a lazy smile as he

watched her slipping on a pair of soft suede shoes. 'He is restless, *cara*. Now that he has seen us settled I think that he has seen the many advantages of married life, and I believe that he intends to sow his wild oats before taking a Sicilian bride.'

From what Emma had heard whispered among some of the women in the family, Salvatore had already sown quite a few! She raised her eyebrows as she lifted her hands to Vincenzo's shoulders and made an unnecessary adjustment to his jacket, but then she just loved touching him. Loved talking to him. Spending time with him. As he did with her. Love had liberated them both and left them free to show how much they cared, without boundary or restraint.

'We ought to go downstairs,' she said, reluctantly. 'The guests will be arriving in an hour or so and there's still loads to do and I want to rescue Carmela from Gino.'

'But everything is ready—you know that—and Carmela would happily take our son home with her given half a chance,' he demurred softly. 'And besides, there is something I want to show you.'

'Oh?' she questioned with a faint frown as he pulled her into his arms. 'And what might that be?'

'First I need to tell my wife how beautiful she is and how much I love her, and then…'

'Then what?' she questioned.

Vincenzo smiled, a smile edged with love and sensuality which Emma had grown to know so well. 'And then I give her…this.'

Emma looked down to see that he had taken a small leather box from his pocket, and in the box was a ring which he was sliding onto the finger of her right hand. Rapidly, she blinked, and not just because it was dazzlingly beautiful—a hoop of diamonds which sparkled like sunlight on the Tyrrhenian Sea—but because the faint glitter of tears in her eyes was threatening to put her waterproof mascara to the test.

'Oh, Vincenzo,' she whispered shakily.

'You like it?'

'I love it—how could I not? But why have you bought it? And why now?'

He smiled, his eyes soft and indulgent. 'Because I love you, in more ways than I can count. Because you are my wife and my soul mate and the mother of my child. Is that reason enough, *cara mia*, or shall I give you more? For I have a thousand reasons at my fingertips and then a thousand more.'

For a moment she felt too choked to say anything and then Emma flung her arms around his neck, holding him so tight, as if she could never bear to let him go—and she never would. Knowing that the love she shared with Vincenzo Cardini burned brighter than all the incandescent stars which hung every night like lanterns in the clear Sicilian sky.

1108/06

Celebrate 100 years of pure reading pleasure with Mills & Boon®

To mark our centenary, each month we're publishing a special 100th Birthday Edition. These celebratory editions are packed with extra features and include a FREE bonus story.

Plus, you have the chance to enter a fabulous monthly prize draw. See 100th Birthday Edition books for details.

Now that's worth celebrating!

September 2008

Crazy about her Spanish Boss by Rebecca Winters
Includes FREE bonus story
Rafael's Convenient Proposal

November 2008

**The Rancher's Christmas Baby
by Cathy Gillen Thacker**
Includes FREE bonus story *Baby's First Christmas*

December 2008

One Magical Christmas by Carol Marinelli
Includes FREE bonus story *Emergency at Bayside*

Look for Mills & Boon® 100th Birthday Editions at
your favourite bookseller or visit
www.millsandboon.co.uk

FREE

4 BOOKS AND A SURPRISE GIFT!

We would like to take this opportunity to thank you for reading this
Mills & Boon® book by offering you the chance to take FOUR more
specially selected titles from the Modern™ series absolutely FREE!
We're also making this offer to introduce you to the benefits of the
Mills & Boon® Book Club—

- ★ **FREE home delivery**
- ★ **FREE gifts and competitions**
- ★ **FREE monthly Newsletter**
- ★ **Books available before they're in the shops**
- ★ **Exclusive Mills & Boon® Book Club offers**

Accepting these FREE books and gift places you under no obligation
to buy; you may cancel at any time, even after receiving your free
shipment. Simply complete your details below and return the entire
page to the address below. You don't even need a stamp!

YES! Please send me 4 free Modern books and a surprise gift. I
understand that unless you hear from me, I will receive 6
superb new titles every month for just £2.99 each, postage and packing
free. I am under no obligation to purchase any books and may cancel
my subscription at any time. The free books and gift will be mine to
keep in any case.

P8ZEE

Ms/Mrs/Miss/Mr...Initials ....

BLOCK CAPITALS PLEASE

Surname ....

Address ....

....

....Postcode ....

Send this whole page to:

The Mills & Boon Book Club, FREEPOST CN81, Croydon, CR9 3WZ